LISA FOX

I was young, I wanted to be a lawyer when ... w up. ...hen I changed my mind because being a famous, yet totally undercover secret agent would be much cooler. I looked into it, but there weren't many job opportunities. I thought for a while and concluded that maybe I should just marry well. People make whole careers of that. I fell deeply in love with Agent Mulder, but he already had Scully, and I don't share.

So, instead, I became a writer. Now I get to be all of those things and so many more.

www.lisafoxromance.wordpress.com

@LisaFoxRomance

A Kiss in the Dark

LISA FOX

HarperImpulse an imprint of
HarperCollinsPublishers Ltd
1 London Bridge Street
London SE1 9GF

www.harpercollins.co.uk

A Paperback Original 2015

First published in Great Britain in ebook format by HarperImpulse 2015

A catalogue record for this book is
available from the British Library

ISBN: 9780008146405

Automatically produced by Atomik ePublisher from Easypress

Printed and bound in Great Britain

I am incredibly blessed to have so many supportive and wonderful people in my life.
Thank you Sara Brookes, Chris Cinelli, Jessie Cinelli, Allison Gibbons, Kacey Hammell, Dori Koch, Peggy Morgan, Jennifer Probst, Fred Urfer, Liia Ann White, Sabrina York
And my editor, Charlotte Ledger, who made this all possible.

Chapter One

The alarm clock cut through Ryan's blackout dreams, and he reached for it from under the covers, slapping it silent. He groaned, opened one eye, then quickly shut it. The morning light was way too bright, like needles in his eyeballs. His next breath awoke searing pain in his chest, which ignited a chain reaction of agony that shot through his shoulders, neck, and head.

"Too early," a groggy female voice grumbled beside him.

Ryan's eyes snapped back open. There was someone in bed with him. He lifted his face off the mattress and slowly turned toward the sound. Every inch of the journey was an exercise in misery. The room spun nauseatingly around, and it took a moment before his eyeballs finally settled in his head enough for him to see the pretty blonde woman beside him. Traces of last night's makeup still rimmed her wide brown eyes and accentuated her high cheekbones. She had a salon tan and a gym body and he had no idea who she was.

She smiled and stroked his face, a gentle caress of her long, acrylic nails. "You were incredible last night."

She grazed his eyebrow, and the flash of pain brought the memories back with razor-sharp clarity. The smell of the gym, sweat and aggression, bright lights on the ring, fists and blood. Three long rounds, a hard-won fight. His opponent was good, he'd made Ryan work for every point. Despite the regulation headgear, he was sure his face had paid some of the price. Then victory, his arms raised high into the air, and the announcement that he would advance to the finals. There was laughter and champagne—his gaze refocused on the woman in his bed—and the Ring Card Girl from the match.

She touched her fingertips to his lips, then rested her hand on his chest. "You're going to be the champion for sure."

Prickles of heat cascaded down his spine as her hand moved lower, tracing the path of dark hair over his pec to the center of his body. The scrape of her nails was intensely erotic, almost too much for his bruised body to handle, and every pleasurable shiver set off another wave of pain. She brushed his navel, but he caught her hand before she could do something he would not want to stop. This was nice and all, but the alarm clock had woken him up for a reason. He had to get to work.

He lifted her hand and kissed her fingertips. "Next time—" His chest seized up. Oh God, what was her name? He didn't know her name! He smiled, trying to cover up the unexpected pause. "—*Darling.*" He kissed her fingers again. "I'd love to stay in bed with you all day, but duty calls, and my landlord is not a forgiving or generous man."

"Call in sick," she said, sex in her eyes.

It was tempting, but Ryan had a firm no ditching responsibilities policy. Drink hard, play hard, work hard. The playing had been fun last night—really fun as he was beginning to recall—but today it was time for work. He threw back the covers and got out of bed to remove any further temptation. The hardwood floor was cool beneath his bare feet, the morning air chilly on his naked skin. He took a deep breath to quell some of the heat sizzling in his blood and bring his body temperature back down to normal.

His nameless lover sat up and the sheet pooled around her waist, offering him a view a man would rightly die for. She was rumpled and tousled and sexy, and the sight of her made him want to seriously reconsider his decision.

She rubbed her eyes with her fisted hands, a gesture both innocent and seductive. "When will I see you again?"

"Two weeks." He needed to get her motivated. He grabbed her top off his dresser, her shorts off the floor, and her panties from the edge of the bed as he circled around toward her. He offered her his hand to help her to her feet. "We'll see each other at the finals." She climbed out of bed, and he handed her the clothing. "I'm going to win it all for you."

She chuckled and Ryan smiled back. He'd had fun last night. He wouldn't mind seeing her again. If there was a next time, he'd be sure to learn her name.

She got dressed and he grimaced. Even in the harsh light, she was hot as hell in that tiny string bikini top, little black short-shorts, and high heels, but there was no way he was going to let her walk to the subway in that outfit in the middle of the morning commute.

"Here," he said, reaching into his dresser. He pulled out a dark T-shirt. "Put this on."

She pulled his shirt on over her head and it came down to around her knees. Good. She slipped her arm through his, and he escorted her to the front door. He had a lot of work waiting for him at the office. His first order of business was to finish the coding on The Candy Connoisseur's website. Then he was sitting in on a meeting about a new client, a swanky new cosmetics company specializing in high-pigment eye shadows. He needed to get himself on that project. If he could sweet-talk the team leader—or even bribe, he wasn't above bribery—maybe…

"Okay, see you then," his companion said, pausing on the threshold. She looked up at him and giggled.

He nodded absently and held the door open for her. He also really needed to update that art gallery's website for one of the other senior programmers like he promised. He couldn't believe he'd almost forgotten about that. Damn. It was going to be a long day.

The Card-Girl lingered in the doorway, and Ryan became slowly aware that she was not moving. He met her gaze and the look in her eye said all that needed saying. She wanted a kiss goodbye. He didn't have the heart to disappoint her. He wasn't a monster after all—just a man who had to get to work. He gave her a nice, long, slow one before sending her on her way.

He shut the door behind her, the memory of her fading right along with the scent of her perfume. A part of him wanted to spin out fantasies of seeing her again, of maybe spending some real time with her, talking and laughing, getting to know one another. Every once in a while, the simple desire to have someone constant in his life made him acutely aware of just how lonely he was. But those thoughts were easily pushed aside. He'd witnessed the reality behind that particular fantasy far too many times to want any part of it. The way he lived now was good. Easy. And that was exactly the way he wanted to keep it.

He turned from the door and headed for the bathroom with a smile on his face. Sure, he hurt everywhere, and the hangover was really beginning to settle in now, but life was good. Really, really good. He indulged in a scorching shower, the hot water loosening his sore muscles. The mirror over the bathroom sink reflected his massive black eye in vivid detail, and he gave himself a jaunty wink while he brushed his teeth. God, he looked terrible.

His face hurt way too much to shave, so he let it go without a second thought. He went back to his bedroom and peered into the closet. He wasn't seeing clients yet, so it didn't really matter what he wore. Today he chose old, comfortable clothes—faded jeans and a navy cotton T-shirt. Thankfully he didn't work in a suit and tie kind of office—unless you wanted to wear a suit and tie of course. Some people did. Ryan was not one of them.

He dressed, reassessing his priories for the day. He couldn't wait for his new-employee probation to be over so he could do some real work, actually build and maintain a website for one of the eclectic and often flamboyant clients Sharpe Designs seemed to attract. That was still a while away unfortunately. When he was hired, he'd been told it would take a minimum of eight months, but probably more, before he got his own solo accounts. As of three days ago, he'd only been there six.

Seagulls were screaming over the Coney Island boardwalk, fighting over the spoils from last night when he exited his building. He said a cheerful good morning to the line of elderly ladies sitting outside the senior center next door, all ready to take in some sun in their plastic lawn chairs with their umbrellas and fans and packs of long, thin cigarettes close at hand. They giggled and waved, just as they did every morning he walked by.

The breeze off the Atlantic Ocean was crisp and invigorating, and he breathed deeply as he headed up the avenue toward the subway. People were already dotting the beach, surfers on the low waves. He passed Nathan's, closed at this early hour, but the scent of the hotdogs ever present in the air. Underneath the aches and pains, his body wanted to move, to stretch, his muscles longing for the daily run along the beach he usually treated himself to. He was a little too late for that today though. He'd run later, when he got home from work. It was just as well. It would be cooler in the evening, and it would give his hangover a chance to subside a bit.

He descended into the darkness of the station and when the subway arrived, he got onboard, squeezing his way into the car with the other commuters. He allowed himself a small grin as he caught another glimpse of his black eye in the reflection of the doors. He'd made it into the finals. He never thought he'd make it that far. He was good, but some of the people he'd gone up against had been on the circuit for years. He was relatively new to the sport and exceptionally new to New York. He didn't know his opponents, had never sparred with any of them, had no concept of their strengths or weaknesses. When he'd signed up for the tournament, he figured he wouldn't make it past the second round, but at least he'd gain a working knowledge to take it all next year. But here he was, getting ready for the finals. It was out of control. He was going to have to call his mom when he got

5

back home. He couldn't wait to tell her.

The train burst out of the tunnel into a blast of sunlight, rumbling over the Manhattan Bridge. The Brooklyn Bridge stood in the distance, lower Manhattan spread out before him. That view always got him revved him up, got his blood pumping. Philly was his home, where he was from, but New York was a pretty spectacular place.

His stop arrived, and he jumped off the train. He exited the station, turned off Broadway, and onto Spring Street. Commuters in suits and jeans, hipster gear and hippy skirts stood on lines for the corner coffee carts, fueling up for the day. He wasn't all that late when he arrived at the converted brownstone that held the Sharpe Design offices, and he congratulated himself on a job well done.

He entered the daily bustle, waving to a few people as he made his way back toward his corner cubicle. The aroma of fresh-brewed coffee hung in the air, and despite his queasy stomach, the lure was too powerful to resist. He needed to check his messages first, then he was going upstairs to the lounge and grab a cup. When he arrived at his desk, he frowned, plucking a Post-It note off the monitor. *Please come see me when you arrive – Ron*, it read, the request written in elegant, flowing script.

Butterflies invaded Ryan's belly. He didn't think he was in any trouble, but a note from the owner was not something anyone wanted to walk in to. He scanned his memory for what he had been working on lately, wondering what he might have screwed up. Nothing came to mind. He tossed the note into the plastic garbage can beside the cubicle and looked toward the polished staircase by the entrance. The only way to find out what was going on was to go up to the top floor and see what the man wanted. He grabbed a notebook off his desk and headed upstairs.

He jogged up, taking two steps at a time, and when he reached the top, he took a left. He passed by a small alcove and a line of executive offices. His sneakers were silent on the lush carpet. Ron's assistant, Mary Ellen, was poised at her desk, lacquered nails tapping away on her keyboard. She was an elegant though hard woman, who took her job as sentry very seriously. If she did not want you to get to Ron, you didn't get to Ron. Even Ron's husband and partner, the CFO, Alan Altman, got turned away. She was not playing. No one was safe. Ryan held his breath while she called back, only exhaling when she waved him inside.

He stepped into the spacious office and smiled when he caught his boss' eye. Ron had the same welcoming expression on his face that he'd had the first time Ryan met him. A little less than a year ago, Ryan had decided to attend a lecture on web design at a friend's grad school in Philly. He'd been discontent with his job, feeling stagnate and bored, and he was hoping for some inspiration, maybe an idea or two on what he could do next. Ron's presentation totally blew him away. The dapper businessman from New York encouraged the students to think about web design as a career choice, not because it was a growing industry or there was the opportunity to make lots of money, but rather because a web designer could actually make a difference in people's perceptions. By designing a person or company's website, your creative vision could and would dictate how people thought of that brand. It was an immense responsibility, but also deeply rewarding. Before Ron was even halfway done speaking, Ryan had already decided he was going to talk with the man that night. Six months later, he was the newest employee at Sharpe Designs and proud of it.

"Oh, good," Ron said, standing up as Ryan entered. His coat was perfectly pressed even though he had been sitting, every hair in place. Ryan felt like a bit of a scrub with his faded jeans and black eye, but it was too late now. He had to just go with it. "I was hoping you'd be in around your usual time this morning." He gestured to the guest chairs in front of his desk. "Please, sit down."

"Thanks," Ryan said, taking a seat. He rubbed his palms together, trying to get rid of the slight clamminess. "What's going on?"

Ron grinned as Ryan sat. "That is a lovely black eye you have there. I hope you won."

"I did." Pride filled his heart once again. "I'm in the finals in two weeks."

"Wonderful! Give the date to my assistant. Alan and I want to come."

"That would be excellent," Ryan said, deeply flattered that they'd want to see him fight. His new coworkers were unlike any he had worked with before. They actually seemed to care about one another. It was nice. Refreshing. "I'd love that."

"Fantastic. We've very excited for you." Ron leaned forward and folded his hands on the desktop. Ryan read the signs and sat up straighter. Small talk was over. It was business time. "I've been very impressed with the work you've done here, Ryan."

Ryan blinked. This was not what he expected at all. "Thank you."

Ron shuffled some papers on his desk, isolated a single sheet, and read it over before meeting Ryan's gaze again. "I think it's time for you to take on clients. I have the perfect one in mind. She's coming in today. In a few minutes, in fact."

Ryan's mouth fell open. Today? No way. He was dressed like a bum, in pain, and worst of all, he was totally unprepared. "I don't know anything about her."

"It's okay," Ron said soothingly, obviously picking up on Ryan's nerves. "It was a last-minute appointment. She was free, and I thought of you. I told her this would be just a consultation. You can go over with her all the things she would've normally filled out online. She's not expecting any results yet."

Ryan's heart sped up in his chest. This was what he had been waiting for since the day he'd started with Sharpe. Finally, the chance to make something functional and beautiful and creative. He could not wait. "Who is she?"

"An author, named Grace Betancourt." Ron flicked the mouse and called up something on his computer screen. "I'm giving you Kat Greer as the graphic artist on this one. Her role will be to set up the designs according to your and your client's specifications, and advise you in any way she can about the general aesthetics."

That was the best possible news. Kat Greer was the company's top graphic artist. She'd won more awards than he could ever dream of even being nominated for. Ron was doing him a huge favor by letting him have her.

"Kat will meet with you and Ms. Betancourt today so she can get a sense of what the client is after and make you up some options to work with, but in the future, you will be meeting with her alone. You'll still report to Dean, and he will advise you, but this is your project, Ryan. Total control."

"This is amazing." He was going to make something incredible for this woman. He couldn't wait to meet her.

"I'm so glad. Kat is expecting you, and I've arranged for you to use The Conservatory for your interview. When Ms. Betancourt arrives, she'll be shown in there."

"Thanks." Ryan always got a laugh out of the names of the meeting rooms here. The Conservatory, The Billiard Room, The Lounge. It may be an upscale firm, but it had a wonderfully geeky heart.

"I know it may seem that sending you out to meet a brand new client with a black eye probably isn't the wisest decision I've ever made, but as I'm sure your coworkers have told you, I have feelings about things. People." He paused, held Ryan's gaze. "And I have faith in you."

Ryan was too blown away to respond. He knew Ron liked him, but this was crazy. He'd never been the kind of person to inspire faith in others. Yes, he was a hard worker, but he was a hard player as well—a fact that never escaped his former employers' attention. He met Ron's eyes once again and nodded to his boss, resolve thrumming in his heart. He was not going to squander this opportunity. When Ron rose to his feet, Ryan mirrored the action, shaking the other man's hand hard.

Ryan left Ron's office, his step light as he headed back down the hallway to the small alcove Kat Greer shared with his direct supervisor, Chief Programmer, Dean Kirkwell.

"Hey, Kat," he called as he ducked into their inner sanctum. The seat beside her was empty. "Where's Dean?"

Kat looked up at him from her desk, her cornflower-blue eyes expertly lined in black. She glanced over at the empty chair. "He's meeting with your BFF in finance. Something about the Fisher account."

Ryan laughed. Gwendolyn Pierce was murder to deal with. She had to be the most negative and cankerous person he had ever met. For no reason he could determine, she mildly tolerated him. She most certainly didn't seem to like anyone else. "Wow, poor Dean."

Kat nodded sadly, but there was a sparkle of mischief in her eyes. "I just hope she returns him to me intact." She sighed dramatically. "I do like him better that way." She grabbed one of the legal pads on her desk. "Are you ready to go downstairs?"

"Yeah." He was bouncing. His first project. He was going to make it great. "Any idea who this person is?"

"No," she said. "A writer. Mysteries, I think. She's got to be close with someone in the Family though. Ron asked me this morning if I could work on this. Appointments never happen that fast and anyone talking to Ron directly has got to be somebody."

He stopped short. She had a point he hadn't even considered. The Family, he'd come to learn, was what his coworkers called the mishmash of colleagues, friends, and lovers that comprised the Sharpe Designs world. If this woman was part of the Family in some way, then this was even bigger than he expected. He really had to make an impression. This was a huge chance. The best kind of nerves jangled his system, very much akin to the kind he felt whenever he stepped into the ring. He was ready to meet this challenge and win.

Kat stood up, taller than usual in super-high, razor-thin heels. He almost wanted to offer her his arm, afraid that she might topple over on the skinny stilettos. Those shoes didn't look like they were meant to hold any weight, but she seemed to manage just fine, walking confidently past him toward the staircase.

Her hips swayed, and he had to work hard to keep his jaw off the floor. The way she moved in those heels and short skirt could do wicked things to weak men. She was everything he liked in a woman—small, blonde, hot, kinda dark and weird. But, alas, it was never meant to be. She was living happily ever after with his direct supervisor. And no matter how hot he thought she was, he could never give her anything like what she had with Dean. Their relationship was a constant source of awe, and if he wanted to be honest with himself, envy too. Sure, he'd show her a great night, but in the end, it would always be just one night. That was the simple reality of his life.

He dragged his gaze away and quickly joined her by her side. If she caught him gaping at her, she'd probably give him another black eye for his trouble. "I saw the latest edition of KLIVE," he said as they descended the stairs. "It was awesome." KLIVE was a gothic-styled web comic Kat wrote and illustrated about a chain-smoking, alcoholic, homicidal bunny working in customer service. He never missed an episode. She had a twisted sense of humor. "But did he really kill Drizz? I can't believe he's gone. He was such a good sidekick."

Kat beamed at him. "I don't know. I haven't decided yet."

They arrived on the first floor and headed for the meeting rooms. The Conservatory was on the right side of the building, a pleasant, airy room done in shades of tan and ivory. A silver tray sat on the conference table with a full French press of quality coffee, cups, spoons, a bowl of sugar packets and artificial sweeteners, and a small decanter of cream. That kind of attention to detail was one of the many things he liked about working at Sharpe Designs, and one of the things that continually pleasantly surprised him.

Kat settled down next to him on the same side of the conference table, their backs to the bookshelves lining the west wall of the room. She pointed to his eye. "Did you win?"

"I did," he said with a grin. He could tell people that all day and never get bored.

11

"Dean and I want to be at the finals. When is that happening?"

"Two weeks. At a gym downtown. I'll email you the details when I get back to my desk."

"We'll be there." She gave him a wide smile. "I can't wait to see you fight."

The door opened, and Ryan and Kat rose to their feet as the receptionist showed in a well-dressed woman. She was tall, probably around five-eight or five-nine, wearing a sleeveless black silk shirt with a scooped neckline. Her long, rich brown hair was pulled away from her heart-shaped face, the ends curling around the swell of her breasts. Her skirt was black and white, simple and elegant, her shoes designer flats.

"Hi," the woman said, leaning over the table to shake their hands. "I'm Grace Betancourt."

Ryan took her hand, instantly captivated by the spray of freckles across the bridge of her upturned nose, the small dimple in the corner of her cheek. Cute, definitely cute. "Ryan Granger." He gestured toward Kat. "And this is Kat Greer."

With the introductions out of the way, everyone sat at the conference table, ready to begin. Ryan caught Grace's eye and a sharp, electric spark of attraction hit him square in the gut. It was a feeling he knew well. Chemistry. And all the right kinds.

"Coffee?" Kat asked, depressing the plunger on the French press.

Grace smiled, lighting up her aquamarine eyes. The color reminded him of the water in the Caribbean, a sight he'd seen on a Spring Break trip long ago. She was very attractive. And in a totally different league than the women he usually hit on.

"That'd be great," she said to Kat and then glanced over at him again. Yes, there was something there between them for sure. He could all too easily imagine breathing in the scent of skin right at the hollow of her throat. She probably smelled of roses, maybe even lavender. "Thanks for seeing me on such short notice. I had to be downtown to meet with my agent today, and I decided to see if you were free." She grinned. "I never expected to actually get in."

That smile just about killed him, and Ryan crossed his legs beneath the table. His priorities were fucked. He needed to refocus. This woman was his client. His first client. He needed to do this right. That wasn't going happen if he spent all his time thinking of ways to sleep with her. He cleared his throat, opened a fresh page in his notebook. "It's great to meet you, Grace. Why don't you tell us a little about yourself and what you're looking for."

"Right," Grace said, hooking her hair back behind her ears. Ryan got a better glimpse of her rounded cleavage and had to quickly look away. "I just signed a new contract for a cozy mystery series—a four-book deal." Her eyes glowed. "I just had a basic website before with my contact information and not much else. But now I need something that's going to attract some serious traffic." She sat up, and there was determination in her posture, a steel in her spine, which only made him want her that much more. "I need to sell some books."

Kat propped her pad up against the rim of the table and picked up her pencil. "Tell me about your series."

"It's called The Georgica Pond Mysteries, and it's about Mia Keller, a former investment banker who leaves Manhattan to open an inn out in the Hamptons." She tilted her head from side to side, seeming to find the description amusing. A tinge of a blush shaded her cheeks. "On the side, she solves crimes."

Kat looked up from her notes. "What kind of body count are we talking about here?"

Grace sipped her coffee, thought it over. "At least one dead per book, but usually it's two. The most I've ever had was six."

Ryan couldn't help but laugh. "That's a lot of people dying in the Hamptons."

Grace favored him with a smile that did terribly wonderful things to his libido. "It's a dangerous place."

Kat tapped her pencil against her lips, a faraway look in her eyes. "The creepiest thing happened to me last night. I don't think I can use it, but you might be able to."

13

Grace put her coffee aside, giving Kat her total attention. "I'm interested."

Kat learned across the table toward Grace. "My boyfriend and I have this wireless printer in our bedroom, one we use mostly for non-work related stuff, so it doesn't get turned on all that often. Last night, in the middle of the night, it came to life. It was probably just updating itself or something like that, but it woke me up. I laid in bed, in the dark, listening to the cartridges scrape and the wheels turn, just like they do right before they're about to print something." Kat gave an exaggerated shiver, but Ryan could see the delighted gleam in her eyes. "While it was doing its thing, I realized I had left my laptop in the living room. All I could think about was what if there was some stranger in the other room, using it to send me some kind of crazy message through the printer. I freaked out a little bit, thinking of the things it might say. Stuff like, 'I see you' or 'You're pretty when you sleep'. I think it would be a great riff on the whole, 'the phone call is coming from inside the house thing'." She held Grace's eyes. "You know what I mean?"

Grace grinned like a mad woman. "That's a really good idea. Maybe not so much the horror story aspect, but maybe the killer could be sending notes, taunting her through the wireless printer. Or maybe he could even send her pictures." She sat back in her seat and nodded. "I like it. Can I steal that?"

"Of course," Kat said. "But you have to dedicate the book to me."

"That's a deal," Grace replied, and the women laughed together. Ryan knew that he should not be fascinated by their conversation. It was morbid and kind of sick. But he liked it. A lot.

"So, the Hamptons," Kat said, picking up her pad once again. "And murder. Is it glamor or is it rustic?"

"Definitely rustic," Grace said.

Kat nodded. "Any themes you use over and over again? Any character traits? Gimmicks? Anything you'd like to see incorporated into the basic design?"

"Just the lake and the B&B. Those things are always in the

stories."

Kat made more notes. The room was quiet as her pencil scraped across the paper. "Okay," she said, finally looking up from her work. "I have another appointment, but I'll get Ryan some mock-ups in a few days for you to look over." She stood up, gathered her things. "It was great meeting you." She circled around the table to stand beside Grace. "I'm going to make you something spectacular."

Grace smiled. "Thank you."

Kat nodded, said goodbye to them both, then left the room.

Grace looked at Ryan and sipped her coffee. Suddenly the pressure was on. He had to make the right impression, but now that Kat was gone, the funky feeling in his gut was insanely distracting. He would be willing to wager a considerable amount of money that she was just as interested as he was. It was loud and clear in the tension in the air between them. But he couldn't act on it. Couldn't even consider it. She was his client.

"So, okay," he said, fumbling a bit. What did he need to know? He looked her over again. Was she free tonight? How did she feel about shameless, hot, animal *sex*? He took a deep breath and bit down on the inside of his cheek as hard as he could. "Let's start with the basics. What kind of pages would you like your website to have?"

"Hmm," she said, thinking it over. "A page for my books for sure. A bio, a contact page, maybe news and appearances? That can be one page." She tapped her index finger against her upper lip and his gaze fixed on her mouth. She was turning him inside out and she didn't even know it. "I think that's it."

He struggled to keep his face professionally plain. "Do you have a fun kind of page? Or a blog? We've found that authors who give readers a little something extra get a lot more traffic and repeat hits."

She curled her upper lip, obviously not liking the idea. "I don't have time to constantly update things like that. I have a tight schedule."

15

Ryan nodded. "I understand. I could do the updating for you, but the information would have to come from you. Quirky things that you've come across while researching, free reads, giveaways. These things really help traffic. It gives people something beyond the basic, 'here's my book, buy my book, please' kind of thing."

She blew air out of her nose. "That does make sense. I'll have to think about it and get back to you."

"Great," Ryan said. "Make me a list and we'll build something from there."

"Have you done this before?" she asked. "You sound like you know what people want."

"No," Ryan admitted. "You'll be my first author." He did not allow himself to fully contemplate the possibilities and implications of that statement. "But Sharpe Designs has a lot of authors for clients, in all different genres. We know what works."

Her smile turned playful, flirtatious. "How'd you get that black eye? An unsatisfied client?"

He laughed. "No, I box." He rubbed his stubbly cheek and the flare of pain was a welcome distraction. "I'm usually more put together than this. Sorry. I was in a tournament last night."

She leaned across the table toward him, offering him an outstanding view of her plump cleavage. "Did you win?"

His mouth went bone dry, and he quickly lifted his gaze up to her face. "I did."

"You must be pretty good."

"I'm very good."

"But not the best?"

He grinned. "I don't like to brag."

She responded with a slow curve of her lush lips. How was he going to get this woman into his bed? That had to happen. Because he wanted her a whole lot.

Her cell phone vibrated, and she jumped. The way she scrambled for it made him think she was expecting an important call. Or maybe dreading one. Her face was tight and tense as she looked at the screen, and then she visibly relaxed. Whatever it was, she decided not to answer it now and tucked the phone back in her purse.

"Sorry," she said, looking back up at him. She took a deep breath, let it out. "I actually need to get going. Is there anything more I can tell you? I have to get my words in for the day."

"I think we're good for now." He wanted to see her again. Needed to see her again. And it was perfectly reasonable. It was for the site. Today was Thursday. He thought about the earliest he could have something done. He didn't want to stress Kat out with a tight deadline. She had at least three other projects going on. "Can we meet again on Wednesday? I'll have a solid working outline for you by then."

She bit her lower lip, looked away. "Do we have to meet? Can't we just do it through email?"

Ryan tried not to take it as hard as he did, but his heart sank as the rejection set in. "Whatever you'd like, Grace. It's your site. We can do it however you want." *But please say you'll meet me, that I'll get to see you again.*

Grace grimaced. "No, never mind, it's okay. I can come in." She gave him a beseeching look. "I just… I have tight deadlines and daily word counts that I have to meet. This is just a bad time." She let out a long breath. "But I guess there never is a good time, is there? And I do want this done. Wednesday is fine. Is the afternoon all right?"

"The afternoon is excellent." Technically, he could do everything by email. But he was selfish and far too happy to let any guilt ruin his good fortune. "How about four?"

She nodded. "Sounds good."

She rose out of the chair, and Ryan held the door open for her as she exited the meeting room. He wanted to offer her his arm, not for support like with Kat, but because he wanted to be close to her, touch her in some way. He couldn't get quite close enough to get a whiff of her perfume and he was intensely disappointed.

He really did want to know what she smelled like.

She left the building, and he smiled to himself as he watched her disappear into the crowd on Spring Street. He was a little pained to see her go, but he would be seeing her again. They had a date. Well, an appointment. Whatever. He was seeing her again and that's all that mattered.

Back at his desk, he sat down and cracked his knuckles. Before he could even begin her project, he had to do a little research on the author. He needed to get a sense of her books, her style, before he could know what was right for her. He tried not to feel like a creeper as he typed her name into Google. It was for work. It was what he would have done with any client. His personal interest had no place in it. The fact that he was thrilled when he saw that she was single meant nothing. She was just another client. He scrolled through the returns, picking up little tidbits about her professional life. She'd won quite a few awards and was part of a reading series last month at The New School. He opened a new tab, went to Amazon, and downloaded her first book to his tablet. He'd read that over the weekend. He went back to his search list and clicked on her Wiki page. It was time to get to know Grace Betancourt.

Chapter Two

Grace flexed her fingers over her laptop keyboard. 4,742 words done. Not the best words, she was going to have to do some serious editing, but still, words on the page. Her gaze flicked to the lower left side of the screen. 31,284 words in total. Not enough. No break for her today. She was writing on a tighter deadline than she had ever worked with before, and she constantly felt like she could fall behind at any moment. She had to make this work, find a way to write more. Missing any one of her new set of deadlines was not an option.

She picked up her coffee mug and blew on the hot liquid, reading over what she'd written. She couldn't go forward until she assessed what she had. There was a new man in town, Seth Winters, and he'd just arrived at the B&B to drop off brochures with deals for the tourists and guests at his new fitness club. He was younger than the heroine, Mia, with dark brown hair and dancing hazel eyes. Tall and fit, Seth was hot, and all the locals and celebrities were flocking to his place to get worked out, slimmed down, bulked up. He had a wide grin with one imperfection, the slightest overlapping of his two front teeth. That tiny flaw in his otherwise flawless face only made him more handsome, and caused the women, and a lot of the men, of the Hamptons to swoon. So far, she wasn't sure if Seth was going to be a murderer or a just another victim.

Or maybe, he could be a love interest for Mia.

Grace rolled her eyes at herself. Could she be more desperate? It was bad enough she'd totally put her new web designer in her book, but to make him her heroine's love interest was going a bit overboard. If she wanted to keep him in there at all, she was going to have to change some of the details. The smile was an especially huge giveaway. Still, Ryan made an excellent model, and Mia did deserve a man. This was going to be her third book and maybe it was time for Mia to meet someone. Readers seemed to like a bit of romance.

Her old leather office chair squeaked as she sat back in it, her feet up on the desk. A love interest would definitely open the series to more people, lend it some new marketability. That was the name of the game after all. She had a four-book deal with advances and publisher expectations. She had to make it good, make it readable and liked. She also really needed the money. She wasn't going to try any gimmick just to sell books, but over the span of four novels, Mia couldn't remain stagnant. That would be dreadfully boring. She needed to have a life in the town. Meeting someone was the next logical step in a normal life. Seth would enrich the story. He was going to have to stick around for a while.

Grace sighed. Not that she could write from experience or anything. Her own life was sorely lacking in the love interest department. Ryan Granger was an attractive man. And if she read the signs right, kind of interested. She couldn't believe she'd flirted with him the way she had. But he'd flirted back. No woman could pass up that kind of encouragement. Her cheeks heated as she recalled his smile, the way his gaze fixed on her, the appreciative gleam in his eyes. It was unfortunate that they met now. She had no time for distractions.

Which reminded her—she had a meeting with him on Wednesday. She needed to make that list of "fun extras" for him. She sat up, opened her calendar, and made a note to do it tomorrow.

She ran her fingers lightly over the keyboard, her thoughts drifting back to her web designer. She was really looking forward to seeing him again. More than she should be. He was a rough sort, the tight, faded jeans, the black eye, the rakish grin. He knew he was attractive too and had no problem flaunting it. His butt had been stupendous in those jeans. She'd bet he'd look good in leather.

Hmm, leather. Leather jacket, leather chaps…

Inspiration slapped her across the face. She sat up, her fingers flying over the keyboard, busting out sixty words a minute. She deleted Seth's original introduction, rewrote his entire entrance. A motorcycle. Ryan—*Seth*—needed to have a motorcycle. What kind of motorcycle? She paused, her hands hovering over the keys. She didn't know anything about motorcycles. It had to be sexy, all chrome and black. She was going to have to ask on Twitter for suggestions. Maybe she should run a contest. Give away a book and allow the winner to decide which bike Ryan—*Seth*—gets to ride. She scribbled a note in the notebook she kept beside the computer, envisioning how she would promote it, getting caught up in the details.

"Okay, stop," she said out loud. Write now, worry about the promo later. She turned her attention back to her work.

Mia frowned at the unfamiliar noise outside the B&B. She peeked through the white lace curtains framing the inn's bay window and watched a man in leather ride by on a (MOTORCYCLE). He parked the bike a few feet away from the entrance, and when he lifted off his helmet, Mia gasped. He was devastatingly handsome, with a thick stock of unruly dark hair, a bold nose, and the kind of lips that could make a woman think about wicked, wicked things. His muscular thighs flexed as he dismounted the bike, and her heartbeat galloped, the blood racing through her veins suddenly a whole lot warmer.

Grace cocked her head to the side, smiling as she read over what she'd written. It was amazing how easy the words came when she was writing about Seth. She was a slow writer by nature and often struggled over every word, but his appearance seemed to flow with a rhythm all on its own. And it was fun writing about him—fun like it had been in the beginning, before she was caught up in word counts and deadlines and marketing strategies. Writing about him brought back the pure joy of simply writing. It was a welcome change—one she hadn't even realized she'd been missing.

She went back to work, the scene playing out in her head as she typed. Seth crossing the spacious front porch, the chime of the bell as he opened the door, the fluttering of Mia's stomach when he approached the reception desk. She gave Mia the warmth she had felt in her own chest when Ryan first smiled at her, that first pulse of instant attraction. Their handshake went on a little longer than normal, and Mia's breath caught as the heat of his palm warmed hers, a wild flush on her cheeks. It was all so clear in her mind, and the words flowed effortlessly, the tension between Mia and Seth building with every new paragraph.

Her phone buzzed, rudely breaking the spell, and Grace lunged for it, her heart thudding in her ears. There was time when she'd keep her phone off for days, lost in the worlds of her own creation, but now the phone was never far from her hand and every buzz made her cringe and jump. A knot formed in her stomach when she saw who was calling, the dread and fear and worry making her physically ill. She slid the bar across the screen and braced herself for whatever bad news the voice on the other end would deliver. "Hello?"

"Ms. Betancourt?" a coolly professional female voice asked.

Grace closed her eyes. Please don't be bad. "Yes?"

"This is Andrea Wilcox from Westview Gardens. Your father has had a very minor accident."

Her stomach lurched, and she clenched her teeth. This could be the nightmare she was always dreading. "Is he hurt?"

"No, not badly. He bumped his head on the way to the

bathroom, and he is understandably upset. I'm sure he'd like to see you." The woman paused. "Of course we were concerned by this incident and we ran some tests. Before you visit him, we'd like to speak with you about altering his level of care. Would you mind stopping by the administrative building when you arrive?"

Grace knew all too well that "altering his level of care" was fancy code for upping the bill. This was the second time since her father had been admitted to the long-term care facility that they'd needed to alter his level of care. Alzheimer's had taken his memory and now it seemed to be taking his basic motor skills as well. When she'd admitted him, she'd wanted to believe they would be able to perform some kind of miracle, maybe help slow down the progression of the disease. Westview Gardens was famous for their recuperative therapies, their brochures boasting they were voted the best residential care facility in the country for five years in a row. If there was any hope for him, it was to be found there. Of course, everything had a price, and in this case, a price no health insurance plan was ever going to pay.

She took a deep breath and rubbed her hand over her forehead in an attempt to soothe away some of the tension. It didn't work, but it was a nice try. Nowadays, she was made of tension. She glanced at the clock on her computer. "I'll be there in an hour."

"That's excellent," Andrea Wilcox said. "We'll look forward to your arrival."

Grace ended the call and instantly went online to the largest car sharing site to see if they had a vehicle free. If not, she'd try somewhere else. She had memberships with all the services and rental agencies. This was not the first phone call she'd received, and she'd learned the hard way that relying on mass transit to get out to Long Island on a moment's notice was not the way to go. With delays and transfers, it had taken her three hours one day to get to her father's side. That was totally unacceptable.

She had luck on her first try and found there was a car available about two blocks away on Riverside Drive. Grace quickly reserved it, grabbed her house keys, and left her apartment. She didn't have time to mess around with makeup or change into better clothing. Appearances did not matter.

It was a beautiful summer afternoon, bright sunny skies, a warm breeze, no clouds, low humidity. The scent of damp earth carried on the wind from Riverside Park, the trees verdant in her peripheral vision. She marched toward the garage, her eyes fixed on the sidewalk. All around her, people were smiling and strolling, enjoying the day and one another. It was the perfect day for a walk, a picnic, a bottle of wine. Sadly, that was not her day.

She got the car—something small and foreign and blue that hadn't been cleaned out by the previous renter. It even lacked a GPS unit, but that hardly mattered. She didn't need one. She knew where she was going. All too well. She brushed ashes off the seat, climbed in, and put the car in drive.

The trip out of the city was uneventful, the traffic sparse. In under an hour, she was pulling into the tree-lined drive of the Westview Gardens Guest Homes and selecting a spot in the visitors' area of the parking lot. A gentle breeze stirred the leafy trees on the campus, birds sang, and elderly people in hospital gowns and robes strolled the winding paths with partners and staff. It was a peaceful place, tranquil, and despite his difficulties, she still felt it was the right place for her father to be. Along with the beautiful setting, they had a nurse practitioner on premises twenty-four hours a day. The staff to patient ratio was outstanding. Everyone had private rooms. If there was a place where he could get better, it would have been here. But despite all the perks, he'd shown no signs of improvement. In fact, everything pointed the opposite way. A lump formed in her throat, and she pressed her knuckles to her mouth to get herself under control. She could not walk in there on the verge of tears. She had to get it together.

She took a deep breath, exited her car, and entered the administrative building. A puff of air conditioning chilled the sweat she didn't realize she'd had on her brow. Her shoes squeaked on the waxed linoleum floor as she walked down the short, wood-paneled corridor. She told the young woman at the reception desk her name and then sat on one of the plush, floral-printed sofas to wait for Andrea Wilcox to retrieve her.

She picked up a random women's magazine and had barely gotten through a thought-provoking article on the proper way to apply eye shadow when a familiar voice interrupted her reading.

"Hello, Ms. Betancourt," Andrea Wilcox said, standing over her. She was an efficient woman in a sensible pants suit, her light-brown hair pulled back in a tight, no-nonsense bun. She looked exactly the same as she had the first time Grace met her, almost two years ago when she'd admitted her father.

Grace stood up and took her hand. "Hello, Ms. Wilcox. How is he doing?"

"He's fine. Of course, we're monitoring him closely, but there's no need for concern. It was just a minor bump." The woman smiled. "Let's go to my office and we'll discuss some of the changes we'd like to implement for your father in the future."

Grace nodded, and Ms. Wilcox led the way past reception, into the right wing of the building. They entered an office at the end of the hallway, featuring a view of the grounds. Certificates and commendations lined one wall, family photos on the other. Grace did not look at any of them closely, her gaze was focused on the center of the large wooden desk, and her father's chart sitting in the middle.

Ms. Wilcox sat in her executive leather chair, put on a pair of wire-rimmed glasses, and opened the folder. She studied whatever was written in there for a few seconds and then looked up at Grace. "I'm afraid your father's condition is deteriorating faster than we'd hoped. We are concerned, but optimistic. However, some aspects of his care will have to change."

"How did he fall?" Condition. Deteriorating. She couldn't process the words, didn't want to. It was easier to focus on something small, something she could handle.

"Unfortunately, he is showing signs of apraxia. He was on his way to the bathroom, and it appears he momentarily forgot how to walk." She glanced at the file again. "Your father is going to require additional assistance in his daily living. His bathing routine for instance must change drastically in order to fit his current needs."

Grace's heart hurt. This disease was the worst thing ever—far worse than even death. "What do you need me to do?"

Ms. Wilcox met Grace's gaze, her expression sympathetic. "I know this is disheartening, but have hope. Your father is in the best care possible, Ms. Betancourt. We will do everything we can to keep him comfortable and safe." She removed a stapled pile of papers from the file and placed them on the desk in front of Grace. "Here are our revised plans. Look them over. We just need your signature to begin implementation." She stood up and walked to Grace's side. "I'll give you a few minutes to review them. Would you like coffee or anything?"

"No, thank you," Grace said, looking at all the small print typed on the stack of papers.

Ms. Wilcox nodded and then left the room.

Grace rubbed her fingers over her eyebrows and then pulled the pile of papers into her lap. Thank God for her new contract. She had his pension and the sale of the house, but that money was only going to last so long. How long would he need this kind of care? Five years? Ten? What if he got worse? Of course he was going to get worse. That's what Ms. Wilcox was telling her. He was only seventy-four. It wasn't inconceivable that he could live for another fifteen years or more. Her new set of advances were nice, but nowhere near enough to support that kind of timeline. She needed to earn more. She was a midlist author at best. She needed to be a bestseller. She had to. Because she was going to need more than just four books now. And the only way that was going to happen was if she sold.

The weight of everything sat on her shoulders, crushed her chest, made it difficult to breathe. One thing at a time, she told herself, trying to hold back the rising panic. It was going to be all right. She *would* make it work. Write the books, promote the books. Make some money. Easy. You can do this.

She lifted the pen Ms. Wilcox left her and began reading the documents. Every place she initialed and signed hurt her heart a little more. This was what her father's life had become, needing his daughter's permission and income to be fed scrambled eggs like an infant.

Ms. Wilcox returned a few minutes later, and Grace handed her the paperwork. "May I see him now?"

"Of course," Ms. Wilcox said. "This way."

Ms. Wilcox escorted her out of the administration building and across the lush grounds to the resident's quarters. Just like in the city, it was a beautiful summer day, but there was no joy in it for Grace.

They entered the cozy brick structure that housed the residents with severe memory impairment, and the smell of old people and hospitals, antiseptics and stewed food, hit Grace all at once, overwhelming her like it always did.

Ms. Wilcox paused in front of her father's room. "We will take good care of him."

"Thank you," Grace said, and the other woman left.

Grace placed her fingertips on the smooth wood door and let out a long breath. It was difficult to see her dad on the best days and today was going to be so much worse. She always wanted to show him a happy face though. He didn't need to worry about her on top of everything else. She made a promise to herself when she admitted him that she would always be positive around him. Lately, it took some real effort to get into the right mind frame.

Once she was ready, she pushed the door open. The old, grey man in the hospital bed bore almost no resemblance to the man she had once known, the strapping fireman who played ball with the neighborhood kids on his nights off. This was not the man who she dreamed was going to give her away at her wedding to the boy next door and visit with his grandchildren on the weekends while she lived her happily ever after.

He looked up and Grace plastered a smile on her face. "Hey, Dad," she said, trying to keep her voice light.

He smiled back, and she immediately knew that this was one of his bad days. His eyes were clouded, distant, his jaw leaning toward slack. She hoped she wouldn't have to explain to him today that he was no longer living in the house in Vermont where she grew up, or that his wife was gone, or who she was.

She crossed the room and pulled a chair over to sit by his side. She took his hand in hers, so frail now she worried she might crush the delicate bones. Her father's hands had once moved downed trees, led men, held her gently, fixed her scrapes and bruises, lifted her up, high over crowds. Those hands were long gone, only a shadow and a ghost remained.

"It's good to see you." She petted the back of his hand and tried not to choke on the words. "I forgot to bring you your maple cookies this time. I'll have them for you next time though for sure."

Her dad made no response, not that she expected him to. He was staring off out the window, miles and miles away from her. She had to swallow hard before she could go on.

"I heard you had quite a day. Maybe you should put aside all that dancing for now." Her lame joke fell flat. "My day was much quieter. I wrote a lot." She tried to think of something to add, but that's all she had done. "Pretty boring, I know, but I love it." She scrambled for more to say. What else was there? There wasn't anything in her life besides writing anymore. "I'm getting a new website. Something really spectacular. Done by a man named Ryan."

She paused. Ryan. Just the thought of him made her heart a little lighter. She glanced at her dad and then quickly away. This was not the appropriate time to be thinking about Ryan. Maybe there was no appropriate time. She couldn't get involved with anybody. Not now. Maybe not ever. "He's really nice."

"You remember the carnival?" he asked suddenly, joyous delight lighting up his entire face. "You loved the cotton candy."

The sudden burst of conversation made her cringe. She had no idea what he was talking about, but she forced a smile on her face nonetheless. At least he was speaking, acknowledging her presence in some way. Sometimes he didn't. "Yeah. That was a great day."

His eyes went hazy again, and Grace bit back the tide of emotion that threatened to gush out of her in an uncontrollable wave. Thankfully, she was saved from having to come up with any further conversation by a white-clad nurse.

"Excuse me," she said, stepping into the room. She held a tray with a number of needles. "Mr. Betancourt needs his medication now."

"Of course," Grace replied, and then turned back to her father. The lump in her throat made it difficult to speak, but she forced the words out nevertheless. "I'll be back on Friday like always, okay?" She gave him a swift kiss on his soft, sunken cheek. Two more minutes, she told herself, you only have to keep it together for two more minutes. "I love you, Dad."

He nodded vaguely, but it was obvious that he was far away, that he hadn't heard a word she'd said. Her heart clenched, but her eyes were dry when she gave the nurse a tight smile and left the room. Keeping her gaze rigidly forward, she walked calmly down the tastefully appointed hallway, out onto the manicured grounds. The rental car beeped when she disengaged the locks. She climbed inside, the cloth seat hot against the back of her thighs. Alone at last, she put her elbows on the steering wheel, buried her face in her hands, and bawled.

Chapter Three

Ryan couldn't believe how nervous he was. He circled the meeting room for the twelfth time, making sure he hadn't forgotten anything. Coffee, cups, condiments, fresh flowers, laptop, notebook, pen. He circled the room again, the opposite way. Everything was still good. He glanced at his wristwatch. Two minutes to four. Grace would arrive any second.

He'd thought about her every single day since their last meeting. During his morning runs, he thought up funny things to say to her, different ways to make her laugh. He reflected on the color of her eyes while crammed on the subway with the other commuters, the memory of the way her freckled nose scrunched up when she giggled heating him up inside. Alone in bed at night, he'd imagined what her skin would feel like against his, how she might close her eyes and sigh into his ear. And when finally he drifted off to sleep, he dreamt of her smile.

His heart skipped when the door handle turned and a wide grin broke across his face as she entered. God, she just lit him up, made him hot and chilled, feverish. She crossed the room, and his first instinct was to take her into his arms, hug her close, and breathe her in, but he refrained. This was a business meeting. He had to at least try to pretend like he was a professional. He held out his hand to her. "Hi, Grace."

She took his hand with a smile. "Hello, Ryan."

Her hand was soft and cool in his, delicate, but also strong, her grip firm. Touching her was like being hit by lightning, an electric shock to all his senses. Getting a woman he'd decided he wanted was never a problem for him, but this was different. Somehow the stakes felt a whole lot higher. He held her hand longer than strictly necessary, making the contact last as long as possible. She didn't pull away. When Ryan finally dropped his hand back at his side, his knees were trembling a little bit. Her effect was insane. He tried his best to pull himself together and gestured to the seat beside him.

She moved around the table toward him, and he held out the chair for her. Today's skirt came down to her knees, a somber charcoal gray and very straight. He wasn't sure why he noticed that. He was not a connoisseur of women's skirts. He sat down beside her, his gaze running from the top of her thigh all the way down to her strappy sandals. It was a lovely view, and he had to forcibly pry his eyes away from her long, slender legs.

"Okay," he said, making himself focus on the laptop's screen. "I'm going to show you a few designs we came up with. You don't have to love the whole package. You can pick parts of what you like from each of them, and Kat will adjust the designs. Once we have a solid working template, I'll build your website around it." He glanced over at her. "How does that sound?"

"Sounds good." She reached into her purse, pulled out a piece of paper. "I got that list of fun things you asked for."

"Great," Ryan said, and placed the sheet next to the laptop. "We'll go over that later." She sat close beside him and he was very aware of the warmth of her body. He was pleased to discover that she smelled like spring, a light, cheerful floral scent. Heat rushed to all the right and very wrong places. He shifted his butt in the seat. Now was not the time to think about how good she smelled. He angled the monitor more toward her, and his knee brushed hers. "All right, here's the first one."

The first image Kat had created filled the screen. It depicted a bright day, sunlight reflecting off the rippling waters of a large lake. On the right side was a rustic-looking inn, almost like a gigantic, multilevel wood cabin. The image was crisp, clean, with lots of white and blue tones. It had a distinctly summertime feel, and Ryan could easily imagine people boating on that lake or enjoying refreshing cocktails on the deck of the inn.

She smiled, but he could tell she wasn't that impressed. "That's really nice."

"There's more," he assured her.

She shifted, her thigh pressing against his under the table, and Ryan's breath caught in his throat.

"Where do these images go? Are they headers? Or will they be backgrounds?"

"Headers," he told her, trying really hard not to concentrate on how near she was, how he could see every single individual freckle across the bridge of her nose. "The list of pages will go beneath whatever image you choose and then we'll create you a front page. That usually features your latest release information, or any upcoming appearances, stuff like that."

She nodded, and he clicked on the next example. It was once again an image of the inn on the lake, but it was done in more a graphic novel style illustration. It was predominantly black and white with slashes of color here and there for dramatic effect.

She leaned closer to the screen. "Wow, that's not what I pictured at all, but I love the drawing."

He made a mental note to tell Kat that later. "Great. That's something we can work with." He clicked for the next display. "This is the last one."

The image showed the lake at night, a million stars in the deep, indigo sky. The lights in the inn were glowing softly, giving it a feeling of warmth. In the distance, there was darkness though, an ominous cast across the wide lake. Something was out there. Something sinister. The juxtaposition between the undefined dark and the comforting light made the inn seem even more warm and inviting, a safe haven in the night.

Grace gasped, her fingers hovering over the screen. "That's the one."

Ryan smiled. "Kat thought you might like that one the best."

"She was right." She returned his smile and his blood ran a whole lot hotter. "You guys do good work."

He almost giggled. Like a school girl. Christ. "Thanks. But this is only the first step. Next, I get to build you something people can actually use."

She practically glowed. "I can't wait."

He could stare at her all day and be just fine with that, but he had sense enough to realize how weird that would be. Reluctantly, he tore his gaze away from her and picked up the piece of paper she'd given him earlier. As he looked over her list, a question occurred to him that had been hovering in the back of his mind ever since they met. "So, how did you get talking with Ron anyway? Do you know him well?"

"No, I've never met him in person. Tennyson Landry invited me to one of the networking salons he does with Sharpe Designs. Marketing for Artists. I'm not the best at promo or publicity, but I need to be. I went to see what everyone had to say. I really liked what I heard, and I let Ten get me an appointment."

"Do you know Tennyson well?" he asked, unable to help himself. The name was oddly familiar, but he couldn't place it.

"We grew up next door to one another. I actually hadn't seen him in a few years. I was surprised when he got in touch. Through Facebook no less!" She laughed and shook her head. "He isn't exactly a social media kind of guy."

Now he remembered. He had met him. Tennyson was that big guy who was dating Stacy Saunders in marketing. What did he do? A painter? A musician? Something like that. "Well, I'm glad he told you about us."

She laid her hand on his shoulder, a light touch that made his skin hum and his clothing way too tight. "Me too."

Sweat formed on his brow, and Ryan wiped it off with a curious frown. Wow, she really did affect him.

Grace waved her hand in front of her face, her forehead creasing. "Are you warm?"

Yes. "Yes."

She cocked her head to the side, listening. "I think the A/C's off."

That couldn't be right. There was no reason the A/C would be off in the middle of the day. But she was correct. Not only was the room hot, it was stuffy too. He got up and went to the door, headed toward reception. Grace followed closely behind him. People were milling about the large foyer, and it seemed dimmer than usual.

"What's going on?" he asked another programmer.

The guy pointed up at the dark lights. "Power's off. Not sure if it's us or a blackout. Maintenance has gone to check."

"Right," Ryan said and walked to the front doors. He looked outside and found people were pouring out the shops and buildings, standing around on the sidewalks looking confused and stressed. The traffic lights were out, but there were plenty of cops on the scene, directing the sudden glut of cars. Some people seemed to be having difficulty getting their phones to work, while others barked and shrieked into theirs.

"Looks like it's more than us," he called back. "Anybody got a radio?"

"I think I can get something," Jodi, the receptionist said. Just about everybody was downstairs now, practically the whole staff gathered around the front desk. She scrunched up her face and did something to her phone. The thing squawked and then male a voice came through loud and clear. "...*give us twenty-two minutes...*"

Everyone burst into applause.

Jodi held up her phone up high over her head. "*Details are still coming in from the tri-state area. New York, New Jersey, and Pennsylvania are all reporting power outages...*"

Someone groaned in the back of the room. "Well, there goes the subway. Looks like I'm walking." Other people grumbled as well, a few of the women complaining they didn't have the right shoes for a power outage.

"*No timeline has been released for when power will be restored. The mayor's office urges…*" the radio host went on.

"All right, people," Ron said, getting everyone's attention with a clap of his hands. "I think we can call it a day. Get home to your families. I know many of you live far. Does anyone need a place to stay tonight? You're all welcome to come home with me and Alan."

"I do," a programmer said. "I really don't want to walk to Hoboken."

"I think I'll get a hotel room," another said. "Stay in the city tonight."

"I don't think a hotel is a good idea," someone else replied. "They're going to be booked. And think how hot it'll be. You can't open the windows in a hotel room."

"Where do you live, Grace?" Ryan asked as people all around them went about making plans.

"West 80th." She looked toward the doors. "I have a long walk. Do you think I can get a cab?"

"Probably not," he said. "I can't imagine there would be any free out there." He touched her shoulder. "I'll walk with you."

"Do you live that way?"

Ryan laughed. "No, I live out in Coney Island."

She shook her head and gave him a dazzling smile. "No, that's insane. You don't have to walk me uptown. I'll be fine."

He thought about the kinds of things that could happen to a pretty woman walking alone in a blackout with all the cops distracted. "No, I'll walk with you."

She shook her head again. "Really, you don't have to. That's an awful long way for you to go, and New York is perfectly safe."

Sure, New York was fine in general, but people often reacted badly when they felt they could get away with it. There were going to be lots of opportunities for mayhem tonight. Without a doubt, there would be looting all across the city, and who knew what else.

There was no way he was going to let her walk alone.

"I like exercise."

She wanted to object again, he saw it in her face, but she paused, and then laughed instead. "Okay, fine. Let's go."

"Great," he said, feeling much better already. "Let me just grab my things and we'll get out of here."

She nodded in agreement, and he bounced away from her, light on his toes. He didn't know why he was so happy. He was going to be walking for miles and miles and hours and hours. But he felt like he'd just won the lottery or something. He dashed back to the meeting room, grabbed his laptop, and cleaned up the coffee service tray. He debated whether or not to bring the computer with him, but ultimately decided he didn't want to carry it around. He dropped it off at his desk, grabbed his keys, and said goodbye to Ron and his coworkers. Everything taken care of, he escorted Grace out the building.

"Let's take Broadway," he said, heading for the avenue. "It'll take us all the way up the west side."

"That's perfect. I live a block off Broadway, between West End and Riverside Drive."

The sidewalks were flooded with people and they wove their way through the executives and tourists, shoppers and drones. Cars were backed up as far as the eye could see and the smells of gasoline and asphalt were heavy in the summer air. Cops stood in the middle of the cross-sections trying to keep the traffic flowing in an organized way. The atmosphere could have been bad, but it wasn't. People were smiling and there was a lot of laughter. Caught up in the good vibes, Ryan took Grace's hand. He thought he might be the luckiest man in the city when she curled her fingers through his.

They dodged a man in clown makeup and costume, laughing together as he passed them by. Grace smiled over at him, showing off those breathtaking little dimples. "Your eye looks much better."

"Thanks. I usually heal pretty quickly."

"Have you been boxing long?" she asked, swinging their clasped hands between them.

It felt good to be by her side, to be holding her hand on this beautiful summer day. He wasn't much of a romantic by nature, but this was nice, perfect in its simplicity. "A few years. Back in Philly"—he glanced over at her—"that's where I'm from, my first job was with an IT company that had a lot of military contracts. Mostly the Marines. One of the sergeants I worked with was an avid fighter. He got me into it. When I moved here, I decided to keep it up. I like it."

She squeezed his hand. "Hitting things is fun?"

"Yeah, but it's more than that. It's a science. It requires strategy, way more than strength. Precision, split second planning, offense *and* defence. It's all about outsmarting your opponent on every level, not just hitting him harder."

"I can see why it would appeal to a military man. Were you a Marine?"

"No way. It was the first job I got right out of college. Great experience, but very regulated." He laughed and shook his head. "I'm not really a regulations kind of guy."

They crossed 8th Street, and he lightly caressed the back of her hand with his thumb while they walked. Her skin was soft, warm. "I think I like it the most though because it lets me be free. There's only the moment, my opponent, my next move. When I'm in the ring, there are no worries, no regrets."

"I know exactly what you mean," she said, looking up at him. "That's what writing is like for me. Immersive and wonderful. It's an escape, but also a destination."

He nodded. He liked that a lot. "The best possible destination."

She nodded back. "Like a tropical island."

"With an open bar."

Her laughter vibrated through his chest. Being with Grace was far better than anything he'd imagined on those long, lonely nights while he was waiting to see her again. Not even his best fantasies compared to the actuality of her presence.

A group of teenagers swept by them, giggling together, the boys trying very hard to get the girls' attention. Grace smiled as they passed. "I love this city. I can't imagine ever living anywhere else."

He felt very much the same. "Are you from New York? You don't sound like you are."

"No, I'm from Vermont. I went to Bennington mostly because my mom was a nurse there and we got a great discount. We would've never been able to afford it otherwise."

Something in her voice was off. "She was? Is she retired now?"

Grace was quiet for a moment. "No, she died a few years ago."

Ryan's heart plummeted. "I'm sorry, Grace."

She shrugged one shoulder. "Thanks. It's better now, but it was hard for a long while."

He wanted to hold her, to comfort her in some way. She looked so sad. "She's at peace," he said, feeling fifty-seven different kinds of lame. He'd never been very good with emotional stuff. He was much better at making a girl laugh then comforting her wounded soul.

"That is what they say." She gave him a tight smile. "And what about your family? Mom and Dad living happily ever after in Philly?"

"Not quite." He really didn't want to get into his family history right then. It was a definite downer and not something to share with a beautiful woman on a gorgeous summer day. He looked around for a distraction and found one almost immediately. "Check it out," he said, pointing across the street at one of the many shoe stores on the avenue. The staff was set up outside, standing behind a long fold-up table loaded with shoeboxes. They seemed to be giving away shoes, handing off boxes to people as they passed by.

"Let's go see what they have," she said brightly. She lifted her foot up and waved her hand over her fashionable sandals. "If I'm going to make it all the way uptown, I'm probably going to need some better shoes."

They crossed over to the store, and Grace got the last pair of sneakers they had in her size—a canvass cheetah print sneaker he was certain the owner was finally glad to be rid of. Ryan had to help her out of the gathering crowd, people with their hands raised high above their heads, groping the air, clamoring for their free pair of shoes. He escorted her away from the teeming masses, keeping an eye out for anyone who thought they could snatch the shoebox from her hands. He glared at the horde, glad he'd decided to walk with her. New York may be safe when there was a cop on every corner, but that was not the case today. He tightened his grip on her hand, and she smiled up at him, completely unaware of his distress. The frown on his face softened when he glanced back at her. It was impossible to be stern when looking at someone so beautiful. She gave his hand a quick squeeze and then released him to lean back against a brick wall to put on her new sneakers.

"What do you think?" she asked, modeling them for him.

She was dazzling in the afternoon light, the sun shining through her chocolate hair, the gleam in her aquamarine eyes, the turn of her calf as she showed him her new shoes. She stole his breath and made him aware of every single beat of his heart. "Stunning."

A rosy flush touched her cheeks. "Thanks."

His gaze fixed on her lips, glossy and slightly parted, and every part of him yearned to know the taste of her kiss. "Here," he said, taking her sandals from her hand. Anything to distract himself from that dangerous train of thought. "Let me carry those." He stuck the shoes in his back pockets.

She laughed as he intended, and he offered her his elbow. She slipped her arm through his and began to walk forward, but he resisted just for the fun of it. Her brow furrowed, and she looked back at him. He smiled at her, a playful grin. Rising to the challenge, she tugged on his arm, but he planted his feet on the sidewalk and wouldn't budge. People streamed around them on their way to wherever they were going and she pulled harder, but she had no real hope of moving him. Her eyes narrowed, and she wrapped both her arms around his biceps and tried again.

"Something wrong, Grace?"

"No. Why would you think there's anything wrong?" she replied, really throwing her weight into it.

Ryan screwed up his face to keep from laughing at her effort. "I don't know, you seem a little agitated."

She chuckled and hugged his arm against her chest. "Are you particularly fond of the view from this spot? Is that why you don't want to move?"

His biceps lay between her breasts and every nerve ending in his body was suddenly on fire. His gaze traveled over her, a sinuous curve from her eyes to her lips, to her throat, to the outline of her breasts pressed again the fabric of her shirt, and then back up again. "It's an excellent view."

She blushed furiously and dipped her head. "You're ridiculous."

"Why?" he asked, leaning down into her space to catch her eye. "Because I think you're pretty?"

If anything, her face got redder. She squeezed his arm tighter and could not meet his gaze. "Stop."

He let her squirm for a few seconds, than relented. "I'll stop. For now."

He started walking, and though she tried to prevent him from moving, he easily dragged her down the sidewalk while she giggled madly.

They walked on, through Union Square, past the Flatiron Building, following the curve of Broadway as it crossed Fifth Avenue and turned west toward uptown. It wasn't long before they could see Macy's and Herald Square in the distance.

"Oh, God," Grace groaned by his side. "I never realized how big Manhattan was before. We're not even halfway there yet!"

"Come on," he said, giving her arm a gentle tug. "Less than fifty blocks to go now."

"Fifty blocks?" she grumbled. "I'm never going to make it."

He nudged her with his shoulder. "You'll make it, even if I have to carry you."

She looked up at him. "Would you really carry me?"

"Sure," he said. "Of course. I could probably piggyback you for twenty blocks without a problem."

She stroked his biceps over the fabric of his shirt, warming the skin beneath. "Are you really in that good shape?"

He grinned over at her. "Boxing requires a lot of training. I take it pretty seriously."

"You're not as big as the boxers I've seen on TV."

"TV loves heavyweights. I'm middleweight. I don't have a big, rocketing punch like the heavier guys tend to have, but I'm quick and I have a long reach."

"Yeah? Is that how you won your last fight?"

"Yes," he said as they entered Times Square. Costumed actors milled around, entertaining the hundreds of people streaming through the center of the city. They dodged Elmo and Pikachu doing a tumbling act for a small gathering of children and couples. Vendors lined the sidewalks, selling water and hot dogs, nuts, candy, and pretzels. "In fact, it got me into the finals. In about a week, I might be this year's champion."

"When's that fight?"

He guided Grace around Captain Hook and out of the heart of the crowd. "Next Friday night at a gym down in Tribeca." He took a deep breath and decided to take the chance. "Wanna come?"

She looked up into his eyes and smiled. "Yes, I would."

He would have never thought three simple words could make his whole day. "I'll leave a ticket for you at the door."

"That's okay, I can buy one."

"We're allowed to have a guest." He held her gaze. "I'd like you to be mine."

She blushed again, and Ryan decided it was his new mission in life to make her do that as often as possible. "Thank you."

Midtown stretched out before them, a never-ending array

41

of luxury stores and overpriced restaurants, tourist's shops and wholesale electronics. Grace touched her throat and looked up at him. "I'm really thirsty. Do you think we can get some water somewhere?"

He looked around and spotted a sidewalk café a little ways up that seemed to be serving food and drinks. "There," he said, pointing it out. "Let's take a break."

She smiled, but then her face instantly fell. "I don't have any cash on me. I doubt they can take cards in a blackout."

"Good point." He rarely carried cash himself. "Let's find out."

They arrived at the café a few moments later and entered the cool, dim establishment. "Hi," Ryan said, to the man standing at the entrance, holding a stack of menus. "Is there any way you guys can take cards today?"

The man smiled. "No problem! We have a card reader on our tablet. We got it after all those brownouts last summer."

"Excellent," Ryan said. He should not have doubted. If there was a way to make money, someone in New York was going to find it. "We'd love a table."

The man showed them to table outside behind the restaurant, a small patio area shaded by large umbrellas. "Our kitchen is all gas," he said, handing them menus. "So, everything is available until we run out." He signaled to someone over their heads. "Your waitress will be right over."

A blonde woman in a long apron approached the table. She was young, probably a few years younger than he was, petite and very pretty. A week ago, he would've been all over her. She caught his eye, and he knew he could have her. Usually that was thrilling, a feeling he lived for, almost like conquering, but today that instinct disgusted him. He was not the kind of man who deserved a woman like Grace. But he wanted to be. More than anything.

"Something wrong?" Grace asked, obviously picking up on some of his internal struggle.

"No," he said, refocusing all his attention on the incredible woman sitting across from him. "Everything's fine."

The waitress greeted them cheerfully. "Can I get you guys anything to drink?"

They both ordered water and settled in to look at the menus. It was a basic high-end diner with specialty omelets and gourmet sandwiches.

"What're you getting?" he asked her.

"Hmm," she said, licking her bottom lip in a way that made his heart race. "I think I want an omelet."

"Yum."

There must have been something in his voice because she looked at him over the top of her menu, then smiled.

The waitress returned with their drink and they both ordered omelets. He got the western, she got swiss and mushrooms.

Ryan picked up his water glass and held it up to Grace. "To blackouts."

She lifted her glass. "To blackouts."

They touched their glasses together and drank. The water was only slightly colder than room temperature, but it was delicious and refreshing. Ryan leaned back in the metal chair, happy with the day. Evening touched the sky, a light dusk of pinks and blue and purple. He turned his face toward the sun, absorbing some of the last rays. Walking miles and miles had never felt so good. But then anything would probably feel good with Grace by his side.

"Feel nice?" she asked.

If only she knew how much. "Yeah," he said. "Real nice."

She looked up at the sky and then back at him. "It's gonna be dark soon. It's going to take you forever to get to Coney Island."

Now that was a hell of a reminder. He didn't quite know why he wasn't trying to scam his way into spending the night in her bed instead of walking all the way back down Broadway and then out to Brooklyn. For some reason, it just didn't feel right. Maybe because she was his client. That had to be it. It was the only reasonable explanation. "I'll be fine."

43

She looked him over, a small smile playing on her lips. "How old are you, Ryan?"

"Twenty-five. Why?"

"I was just wondering." She met his gaze, her face serious. "I'm older than you."

Yeah, by maybe three or four years at the most. She was so earnest, he had to mess with her a little bit. "Well, you don't look a day over fifty-six."

She laughed and slapped his arm. "I'm going to be thirty in October."

She said it rather primly. It was cute. "Dear, God," he said, grabbing his chest. "You're ancient."

She shook her head. "You really are ridiculous."

"My lady," he said, sitting up to take her hand. "I do it all for your pleasure." He kissed her knuckles and that blush he liked so much once again stained her cheeks. He really did enjoy seeing it.

The waitress arrived with the food and they dug in. He hadn't realized how hungry he was until he took the first bite. The omelet was exceptional, a melody of flavors that exploded on his tongue and hit his taste buds just right. She must have been hungry too because they passed the rest of the meal eating in comfortable silence.

Chapter Four

"All right," Grace said as they stepped out of the restaurant. People streamed up and down Broadway in singles, pairs, and groups, young people and old, all enjoying the day and one another. She looked north, squinting as the fading sunlight blazed in the corner of her eye. "Only about twenty-five more blocks to go."

"Are you ready for that piggyback now?" he asked.

She chuckled and shook her head. She couldn't remember the last time she had laughed as much as she had today. He was truly ridiculous. She had no doubt he would piggyback her all the way home if that was what she wanted. She thought of how silly she would look climbing on his back. How it would feel to wrap her legs around his waist, have him between her thighs, her arms around his neck, holding on tightly…

"Let's cross the street," Ryan said.

Grace looked back over her shoulder to see some kind of disturbance happening a few yards down on 62nd Street. It looked like there was a bunch of people gathering around outside a store. The sound of breaking glass was very loud and then alarms pierced the otherwise quiet evening. Even as she watched the scene unfold, she couldn't quite believe what she was seeing. "Are those people *looting*?"

He nodded. "Yeah, I think so."

Her mind had a hard time processing that people were looting on the Upper West Side. It was disturbing in a way she had never considered before. She moved a bit closer to Ryan, and he put his arm around her shoulders. She wound her arm around his waist and hugged him tight, suddenly very grateful for his company. People really did go primal at the first opportunity. The West 60's was a high-rent district, full of cute specialty stores, organic markets, and tea shops—not the kind of place where you'd think to find looters. But maybe she was dreadfully naive. The lights go out and people start ransacking precious little doodad places not because they need anything, simply because they could. There were probably going to be lots of crimes of opportunity committed tonight. Maybe even crimes like murder.

"Hey, Grace," Ryan said, breaking into her thoughts. He gave her a gentle squeeze. "Still with me?"

She shook herself out of her daze. "Sorry. I was thinking maybe there would be a blackout in my next book. Maybe people would go a little crazy in the Hamptons and murder would occur."

He laughed. "Feeling inspired, are we?"

The vibration of his laughter rumbled through her, tickling her insides and heating her cheeks. "I am. I'm thinking the lights could go out and people would freak. Old animosities stir and murder becomes a possibility."

"Vengeance and opportunity."

"Exactly."

He smiled over at her. "I like it. I have to tell you, I really enjoyed your first book."

She blinked. "You read my book?"

"Of course I did. How could I make you a website if I didn't know your work?"

"Oh," was all she could manage. This could be bad. When she started writing Seth, she didn't think Ryan would ever read it.

"Yeah," he went on, oblivious to her discomfort. "I can't wait to read them all."

She bit the inside of her cheek to keep from cursing. She was too deep into the story and the character to change him now. Plus, she liked Seth. He was developing really well. And Mia seemed to like him too. An awful lot. Maybe Ryan would get bored. Or maybe when the job was done he'd forget. Which reminded her of the whole reason she was with him at all. "I really liked the way that last website image looked. But maybe the inn could be a little bit brighter? Maybe even more in the forefront?"

Ryan nodded. "That isn't a problem. We should meet again and discuss some more details on how you want the pages set up and what kind of content they're going to have."

Yes, she definitely wanted to meet with him again. "When is good?"

"When is good for you? I can work with your schedule."

Today was Wednesday. No words in today. That was a problem. It meant she had to do double on Thursday. Her laptop was charged, so she could write if the power was back on or not during the day, but she hoped it would be back by tomorrow night at the latest, or else she was going to be working in the dark. And then Friday was a bust 'cause it was the day she saw her father, and she could never write on those days. On that day, she went home and had a drink. Sometimes two. Friday night, she watched movies, read books, went to bed. Anything to not feel what she felt after those visits. So, that meant a heavy weekend and lots of editing *and* new words on Monday. Her head started to hurt and she had to push the panic down. This schedule was killing her. "How about late Tuesday afternoon?"

"Tuesday afternoon is just fine."

A group of young women passed, all of them around Ryan's age. He took one quick look at them and then returned his gaze to her. There was something in his look though, something sleek and sharp, which made Grace wonder if her sexy, young web designer wasn't a bit of a playboy. She'd had the same feeling at the restaurant, when their pretty, blonde waitress approached the table. A part of her just knew that if she wasn't by his side, he'd be talking to those girls right now. Jealousy made her want to grimace and spit, but she held herself in check. As much as she liked his company, he didn't belong to her. He had the right to do whatever he wanted when she was not around. And while everything she told herself made perfect, logical sense, it didn't stop a bitter worm from squirming in her heart.

Night was setting in as they passed Lincoln Center, the fountains off for once. No water show was happening tonight without the power on. They passed a group of people gathered around an old Plymouth, the car radio broadcasting up-to-the-minute news bulletins.

"*Power outages have been confirmed all along the eastern seaboard,*" the radio announcer said. "*There is still no timetable on when power might be restored. 'We're waiting on Canada,' a spokesperson said at a conference held an hour ago at the...*"

"Sounds like there won't be any power tonight," Grace said.

Ryan looked up at the darkening sky. "I guess not."

"Blackout party on the roof of 50 Central Park West!" a man in the crowd yelled. He was dressed in stereotypical hipster fashion— skinny jeans, ironic T-shirt, thick mustache. "Warm beer! Twenty bucks a person. Cash only!"

A few of the younger members of the crowd expressed interest in going.

"Wanna go to a rooftop party?" Ryan asked her.

She scrunched up her nose. "I think I'm a little too old."

"Right," he said, drawing out the word. "I forgot. You're ancient."

She laughed and touched his shoulder. He had a great body. Hard and strong. "Also, we have no cash." The crowd broke up, a number of them going off with the hipster guy and Grace watched them go. "It's probably just a scam to get everyone up there and kill them all anyway."

Ryan chuckled as they continued on their journey. "You really are a morbid woman."

"Yes," she agreed. "I am."

They walked the last few blocks in compatible silence, watching the night come on and people pass them. "You know, it's probably been over a year since I've been to any kind of party at all."

He frowned. "Why's that?"

Why indeed. She never did anything anymore. Once she belonged to a writing group, had friends that she met for coffee and lunch. Every now and then she even dated. Now all she did was worry. And write. And then worry some more. "I have a lot of responsibilities."

"I can understand that, but you gotta make some time for fun. Otherwise you're only living half your life."

That may be true, but lately, she felt like she had far too much of a life to handle. She glanced over at him and then quickly away. It didn't matter how much she might want him, if she attempted to add one more thing to her tight schedule, she feared she might break. "Old ladies have bedtimes, Ryan," she said with as much cheerfulness as she could muster. "The blood of virgins is hard to come by nowadays. We need our beauty rest."

He laughed and pulled her closer, the warmth of his body a bittersweet comfort she foolishly savored while they walked ever onward.

They turned west on 80th and soon were standing in front of her building. Her street seemed unfamiliar and wild in the dark. Usually there was very little activity outside, but tonight people were gathered on the stoops, playing music, talking and laughing. She looked up at the sky and smiled. The night was ablaze with light, stars and constellations she could not name. "I don't think I've ever seen so many stars in New York City before."

Ryan looked up with her. "I think you're right. Is it too bright, you think? Or is it that we never look up?"

A very valid question. She couldn't remember the last time she'd looked at the sky. "A little of both, I guess."

His arm felt good around her shoulders, and they stood together, enjoying the rare and spectacular view. There was such simple pleasure being by his side, staring at the stars. Contentment she had never known before blanketed her with an inner quiet. A sense of peace. She leaned into him, and his arm tightened around her. She breathed in his clean scent and felt at home.

"Look," she said, pointing to the sky. "Is that a falling star?"

"It's a comet named Endymion," a little girl said from the next stoop over. "They called it that because it passes so close to the moon, but never touches it."

Her mother smiled at them apologetically. "She just went to the Hayden Planetarium on a school trip yesterday."

"I'm going to be an astrophysicist like Neil deGrasse Tyson," the girl told them.

Ryan smiled. "That is an admirable goal."

Grace looked back up at the comet and then over at Ryan. She did not want the evening to end. Not yet. And maybe not all of her reasons were chaste. "Do you…?" She blushed, looked at the ground, took a deep breath. For once, she had to go for it. The night was a bust. She wasn't going to get any work done. Maybe she could steal this one little minute for herself. She met his gaze again. "Do you want to come up and have a glass of water or something before you go? You've got such a long walk ahead of you."

A wide smile broke out on his handsome face, and Grace was afraid she might actually swoon. "Yeah. I'd love to have some water."

"Good," she said, a crimson flush heating her cheeks. She hated that she blushed so easily. Hated that it showed. She jerked her thumb toward the building. "I live on the fifth floor."

He gestured her ahead. "Lead the way."

He climbed the stairs by her side, his hand resting lightly on her lower back. The warmth of him penetrated the thin material of her shirt and quickened her steps. Her heart rate picked up and even though she knew she was being foolish, she couldn't but feel a little giddy from all the possibilities her overactive imagination could dream up about having him in her home.

They arrived at the door, and she let him into her one-bedroom apartment, praying she hadn't left any underwear lying on the couch or something equally embarrassing. Thankfully it was a little too dark to see anything, but nothing seemed too out of order in the living room. The sofa was free of undergarments, and her desk was in reasonably good order. She took a quick glance to the left, toward the small kitchen area, and breathed a sigh of relief. No dishes in the sink. She was a better housekeeper than she thought. She reached for the light switch, but of course nothing happened when she flicked it on.

She put her hands on her hips and looked around the dark room. "I guess we need candles."

"Do you have any?"

"I do. Somewhere." If only she could remember where she stuffed them. It was a sad comment on the state of her life that she had no real use for them. There was no reason for her to have them around, no romantic moments to savor, no candlelit dinners to linger over. "Have a seat," she said, waving him toward the couch. "I'll be right back."

"Can I help?"

"No, I got it. It'll be better if we're not both stumbling around in the dark."

He headed for the sofa, and she made her way toward the bedroom, walking slowly to not bump into anything. She automatically flicked the light switch on when she entered the room and cursed herself for being an idiot. She pulled open the closet door and gazed into the darkness. This was not going to be a fun hunt. She groped around blindly and found a large box in the far back corner, the place where she tossed all the sparkly doodads and other assorted items she kept for no good reason whatsoever. Her hand closed around a long, tapered, wax wand, and she smiled. She located another one and pulled the candles out of the box. She recalled receiving them as part of a goodie bag from a wedding last spring, and she held them up to read the names of the bride and groom engraved on the side. Thanks Todd and Jenny, she thought, and left the bedroom behind.

"Got a light?" she asked when she re-entered the living room.

"Nope," he said, shaking his head.

"Okay," she said and went back to the kitchen. She found some matches in her utility junk draw and lit the wicks. They brightened up the room which was great, but what was she going to do with them now? She didn't own anything that even remotely resembled a candle holder. At a total loss, she grabbed a dish, dripped some wax on it, fastened the candles in place, and hoped for the best. She carried the dish back into the living room and placed it on the coffee table.

"Nice candle holder," he said.

"No one likes a smart ass, Ryan," she said, blowing an errant strand of hair out of her eyes. She watched the candles for a second to see if they were going to remain upright. They seemed okay, so she nodded to herself, a job well done. "Okay, part one complete. Now we need some water."

"Are you sure I can't help you?"

"No, I got it."

She patted his knee and went back to the kitchen. The candles cast just enough light for her to see into the cabinets. She pulled down two glasses and went to the refrigerator. The pitcher of water she kept in there was still cool. She poured them both a glass and carried them back into the living room.

"Thank you," he said when she handed him a full glass.

She flopped down on the couch beside him. "Wow, that was a lot of work."

Ryan laughed, imperfectly perfect white teeth flashing in the golden light. She wasn't used to being around a man as attractive as he was. She generally dated geeks, professors, quiet engineers. Not younger, hip, web-designing boxers. She met his gaze, the candlelight reflecting in his dark eyes. Her cheeks heated once again, and she couldn't help but giggle.

"What?" he asked, a smile touching his lips.

She shook her head and leaned back on the couch, melting into it. It felt so good to sit down. "That was the longest walk I've taken in my *whole life*."

"Aren't you from Vermont? Didn't you have to walk miles and miles uphill in the snow to school?"

She shook her head in amused bafflement. "They do have cars in Vermont, you know."

He shrugged. "If you say so." He touched her thigh, a gentle, fleeting caress that sent shivers over every inch of her skin. "We probably only walked about five miles though."

"Really?" She toed off her hideous, but very handy sneakers. She was grateful for them, there was no way she could've made that walk in sandals. He would've had to carry her for real. She tucked her legs underneath her, massaging her tired calves. "God, it felt like a million. Why'd it take so long?"

Ryan laughed. "'Cause we were walking at like zero miles an hour." He poked her side, teasing her. "We weren't even walking. We were strolling. Meandering. Ambling, even."

She tried to give him a pouty face, but it was hard when all she wanted to do was smile. "Are you making fun of me?"

He nodded, then reached out to brush a lock of her hair behind her ear. "A little bit."

Her eyes flicked to his lips and wonderful bubbles of attraction boiled up within her, like freshly uncorked champagne. "That's not very nice."

He traced the curve of her cheek with his index finger. "I'm not very nice."

Something in his gaze made her pause. The words were said lightly, but there was more there. He was kidding, but maybe not entirely joking. It was a thought to meditate on another day because he moved in closer, or maybe she was the one who moved, she didn't know, all she knew was that she was lost in the dark pupils of his eyes, in the scent of his skin, his shampoo, his clean cologne. Her gaze lingered over the bow-shaped curve of his lips, the dark stubble framing his mouth. "That's too bad. I tend to prefer nice guys."

"Do you?" The breathlessness in his husky voice made her tingle in all the right places. He nuzzled her nose, gently nudging her chin up and when his lips brushed over hers, everything in her went liquid. "Are you sure?"

Electric sparks raced down her nerve endings, heat exploding in her veins. He cupped her face, and she leaned into his palm, his caress. Her heart hammered in her chest, her pulse off the charts. When his lips met hers, she opened for him instantly, hungry for the flavor of his kiss. He slipped his tongue into her mouth, and she moaned, relaxing her jaw to let him all the way in. His soft grunt of satisfaction lit her insides aflame. She shivered, hot and chilled, hypersensitive to his touch. He teased her with light nips and nibbles, alternated with hard thrusts. She lost herself in him, in every gasp, every pounding beat of her heart, and she melted into his arms, giving herself over to him entirely.

They met and parted and met again, a long, slow kiss that heated every single cell in her body. He caressed the line of her jaw with his thumb as they connected in the candlelight. His lips were firm yet yielding, stroking and tender. He drew her closer, his hard chest pressed against hers. Her fingers tangled in his short, thick hair as she invited him in deeper.

A flash of light caught her off guard, and she flinched, automatically pulling away from him. Every light in her apartment came on, and she was blinded by the sudden brilliance. Dazed and disoriented, she looked around the room, trying to acclimate to the brightness. Her gaze touched on her desk, the TV, the old-fashioned digital clock blinking midnight over and over again.

"Looks like the power's back on," Ryan said, squinting in the light.

"Yeah, I guess so."

Cheers came from outside, and she laughed along with the

people on the streets. She tingled from his kiss, the taste of him still on her lips. She felt light, giddy, her cheeks were flushed, and for the first time ever, she didn't mind. She glanced over at him and though her body screamed for more, good sense prevailed. She had things to do tomorrow. "At least you won't have to walk now. The subway will be back in service."

He nodded once. "You're right. It's probably late. I should get going."

They both glanced over at the clock, but it was no help, it was still blinking midnight. He stood up, and she walked him to the door, where they paused for a moment. He took her hand, gently caressing her fingers. "I want to see you again."

She smiled up at him. "You will, on Tuesday."

He shook his head. "No, not at work. Let me take you to dinner." He brushed a lock of hair off her shoulder. "Tomorrow night."

She wanted to, more than anything, but she had responsibilities. Tonight was fun, but too much indulgence was not something she could afford. "I can't, Ryan. I'm on a tight deadline. Please understand." She needed him to understand. "I'll see you Tuesday, and we'll do something after our meeting." It was a consolation prize and she knew it, but that way she could see him on a day she'd already budgeted for not writing and be able to enjoy his company guilt-free.

He looked pained. "I probably won't be able to leave right away. After you approve the site, there will be things I have to do. You'd have to wait around for me."

"I can do that," she said, placing her hand on his chest to comfort him. "I can find things to do in SoHo. Trust me."

He still wasn't sold. "If you're sure…"

"I'm sure." She wanted to be with him, more than she had wanted anything else in a long, long time, and she might be able to make it work if he didn't ask for too much, if he let her make their schedule. There would come a time when he would want more, it was inevitable, she knew that, but for now, maybe he'd just let her see him when she could, when she could make the time. Getting involved with him was going to be dangerous, but if he didn't push, she might be able to keep everything under strict control.

"Okay," he said. He dipped his head and kissed her lightly on the lips. "Goodnight, Grace."

She smiled and touched his cheek. She was a lucky woman. "Goodnight, Ryan." She stood in the doorway and watched him walk down the hallway, then disappear down the stairs. Her heart ached a little when he was finally out of sight, the empty space in her chest she'd ignored for so long suddenly demanded to be filled. She closed her door with a sigh, and though she tried to avoid it, she went to bed dreaming of his kiss.

Chapter Five

The cursor blinked in the corner of the blank page on Grace's laptop screen, but she was staring out the window, her mind far away. She could still feel the sensation of Ryan's mouth on hers, the taste of his lips. She closed her eyes and chills ran down her spine as her body relived its reaction to his touch. She'd spent far too many hours already imagining what could've happened if she had not sent him away that night, all the ways he might have touched her, but she indulged in one more illicit little fantasy, this one involving a slow strip tease.

Her phone buzzed, and she snatched it up to see who had texted her. It turned out to be a spam ad, and she put it aside with a disappointed sigh. It was corny, but she reveled in every text she'd shared with him since the blackout. Not that they talked about anything exciting. Their conversations were completely mundane—they discussed work and their day and shared nonsensical little tidbits of information. But however ordinary, she'd been thrilled every time her phone buzzed with his reply, and she'd saved every single one of his messages.

She glanced at the blank page on her computer screen and a quick tinge of guilt pierced her bubble. She needed to get some words in today. But thoughts of Ryan were so tempting, so self-indulgently easy to slip into and get lost in. With the way things had been going lately, she was ahead of schedule. She would not miss her deadline. Besides, wasn't a girl entitled to think about the boy she liked? Especially when he liked her back? And she thought he did like her back. She wanted to believe it at least, believe that his smile was for her alone, that his kiss meant something more than just a kiss.

She pressed her fingers to her lips and smiled. She had never in her entire life kissed anyone like she had kissed him. Her skin still tingled just thinking about it. She thought she had kissed people with meaning before, but she was wrong. A kiss was more than just a gateway to other things, it was its own separate, special thing. And very precious.

She blushed remembering the look in his eye when he told her he thought she was pretty. It was a silly, offhand compliment, she knew that, but it still made her feel all gushy inside. He made her feel all gushy inside. And he was a good man, smart and confident. He might be younger than she was, but he had his act together. He'd be fun to date—if she had the time for such things. Which she didn't. She knew that. But it was nice to think about. Where would he take her? Places she was sure she'd never heard of. And she'd get to be with him again, kiss him again, touch his amazing body. She bit her lower lip, heat rising from her core. She was absolutely certain he'd be really good in bed. Caring, but a little rough, playful and aggressive.

Suddenly the room seemed very hot, and Grace sat up in her chair, blinking away the foggy blanket of her thoughts. Now was not the time to fly off on that particular fancy. She looked at the computer clock. Two hours until her appointment with him. Two hours until she saw him again. She wanted to shiver and giggle, but she set her spine instead. Two hours to *work*. She lightly tapped the keys beneath her fingertips, not hard enough to actually type anything, and willed herself back into the story.

Mia spotted Seth sitting on a bench across the lake. A breeze ruffled his dark hair and her heart picked up a bit. She was only vaguely aware of the goofy smile on her face when she raised her hand to call out to him, but paused, the smile dying on her lips when a man she knew all too well sat down beside him. Colin Mayor was rich, handsome, and had the blackest heart of anyone she had ever met—which was saying a lot since she used to work on Wall Street. The men put their heads together, and Mia frowned. Now what could those two be talking about?

Grace nodded to herself. Mia liked Seth—there was no doubt about that—but she didn't quite trust him yet. Seth was firmly on Mia's side, but she couldn't see it because she was too busy being suspicious. Mia would continue to doubt him throughout this book, but Grace had already plotted it out that Seth would prove his devotion when Mia needed him most. Of course, she was going to be less than thrilled with his interference, but her heroine was just going to have to deal with the dashing new man in town, no matter how much he annoyed her.

Mia and Seth had a real future together. She could already imagine them in the next book, forced to work together to solve the blackout mystery. Seth was in the Hamptons to stay. Her fingers flew over the keyboard, giving life to the voices in her head.

Her palms were clammy as she rode the subway downtown to Ryan's SoHo office. The train stopped at Columbus Circle, the doors opened, people exited and entered the car, the doors slid shut. Grace took a deep breath and smoothed down the front of her summer dress. She needed to be professional. This was a business meeting. She could swoon all she wanted when they went to dinner later.

Dinner. A date. The words made her smile. She'd done her work for the day, and she had earned this reward. She loved

59

writing about Seth, loved imagining his developing relationship with Mia. This book was turning out to be one of her favorites. Maybe even her most favorite. It wasn't even finished yet, and she was already thinking about the contests she wanted to enter it in. She wanted to believe that this was the book she had been dreaming about writing, the breakthrough novel that would put her name on all the best seller lists. Even if it wasn't, the joy of writing it was enough to alleviate some of the pressure she'd felt recently, and that alone was a miracle.

She headed out of the subway at Spring Street and strolled down the couple of blocks to the brownstone, happily lost in her plans for future chapters, future books. When she entered the office, the receptionist greeted her and escorted her to the meeting room. Ryan was already there, seated at the conference table. Their eyes met, and her heart did a funky little skip-thump in her chest.

"Hi," she said, grinning like a lunatic. How was it possible for him to look better every time she saw him? No man had a right to be this sexy. Today he was wearing a periwinkle button-down shirt that flattered him beyond belief, bringing out the twinkle in his hazel eyes. His tight jeans left very little to her imagination, and she had to pry her gaze away from all that he had to offer and force herself to focus on his face.

He returned her grin. "Hi." He walked over and drew her into his arms for a big hug. "I missed you."

His body was warm, firm, just as good as she remembered it, and a wild blush spread over her cheeks. "You're ridiculous."

"You keep telling me that," he said, and escorted her to the open laptop. He held out a chair for her and rolled it under the table when she sat. "But I'm only telling you the truth."

Flirting with him was fun, but no matter how much she enjoyed it, she took it all with a grain of salt. He was smooth, a total charmer, and she was certain he'd told many other women much the same nonsense in the past. She just had to remind herself not to take him all that seriously, otherwise he'd be very dangerous indeed. She gave him one last smile and then nodded her chin toward the laptop. "What do you have for me?"

His glance almost melted her panties. "I think you're going to like it."

She moved her chair closer to his. She could smell his cologne, his shampoo, and she breathed in a little deeper. He was intoxicating. "Show me."

He touched the mouse, and the computer screen came to life. Grace gasped. The header rested on the top of the page in all its dark and welcoming glory. The front page featured a glossy image of her latest release coupled with the blurb and some quotes from her better reviews. The fonts were bold and stylized, easy to read and classy. It was better than anything she could have ever imagined. She reached over and placed her hand over his. "Show me everything."

He did as she asked, giving her an in-depth tour of all that he'd created for her. He was like a kid as he clicked through the pages, and she only liked him more for it. His excitement was contagious, and she was ecstatic with everything he showed her, listening to him explain all the details of how and why he decided to add what he did, even though she only understood about half of it. When she called Ron for an appointment, all she'd wanted was something to help her sell some books. But Ryan had given her books life. He'd given her something of real beauty.

"Do you like it?" he asked.

"Ryan, it's outstanding."

"I'm glad."

"Thank you so much." She met his gaze. A simple thanks wasn't enough to convey how grateful she was to him, how moved she was by the quality of his work, and the effort he'd put into making the site for her. It was a shame she was so much more eloquent in text than she was in real life. If this had been a scene in one of her books, she'd be able to express her feelings with elegant grace. Sadly, thank you was going to have to do. "So, what happens now?"

"I need to do some final coding, and then we'll get you set up on a host. Once that happens, your new site goes live. It'll come up in all the various search engines and people will start visiting it. We'll send you quarterly reports so you can see how much traffic your site is getting and where it's coming from. Marketing has a whole plan set up for you, so expect a lot of hits. Your agent will send us any events or appearances you're doing and your new release information, and we'll keep that all up to date for you. Ideally, every three months or so, I'd like you to send me some new free content for your readers so the site stays fresh." He smiled at her. "And that's pretty much it."

She did an excited little chair dance squirm. "I have a website."

He nodded. "You do."

She laughed. "You know, when I started writing seriously a few years ago, I never thought I'd be here."

"No?"

"No. I mean, I have a website. I sell books. People I've never met read my work. And they enjoy it! It's beyond a dream. I'm so lucky." She looked at him and shook her head, once again at a loss for the right words to express herself. "Do you ever feel that way?"

"Oh, yeah," he said. "My wildest dream when I was a kid was to have a house on an ocean somewhere and be able to eat takeout every day." He laughed. "Now that I think of it, I'm actually living that dream right now. My life is insanely good." He reached over and took her hand. "And it's only gotten better since I met you."

A blush scorched her cheeks. "You're—"

"Ridiculous?" he finished.

"Yes," she said, twisting her fingers around his. Warmth spread through her chest, making her limbs feel tingly and light. This was a brand-new feeling for her, and she rather enjoyed it. "Where are we going to dinner tonight?"

"Something in the area maybe?" His brow furrowed, and he glanced at his wristwatch. "I have to meet with my supervisor and tell him you approve, and then—"

She touched his shoulder, halting his tumble of words. "It's okay. I understand. I have stuff I need to do while I'm down here. What time should I come back?"

He hesitated. "Can you give me an hour and a half?"

She rose to her feet. "That's perfect."

He walked her to the door, but instead of opening it for her, he thumbed the lock.

"What are you doing?" she asked, a smile creeping across her lips.

Her breath caught as he stepped closer, the heat of his body on hers. "Do I get a goodbye kiss?"

She decided to tease him a little bit. "This isn't goodbye. I'll be seeing you again in about an hour."

He dipped his head and caught her lower lip between both of his, a light though thoroughly sensual peck. "But I'll miss you so much." He nuzzled her cheek. "I need something to hold me over until I get to see you again."

Helpless, she was completely helpless against him, against this... this *thing* they had. She wrapped her arms around his neck, her fingers twining in his hair. "I'd hate for you to be depressed while I'm gone."

He touched his nose to hers, his breath warm on her lips. "I'll be very depressed. Practically inconsolable."

God, he set her on fire. Being with him was fun, but her physical need for him was out of control. Her body craved his, her thoughts consumed with being close to him. And though she knew it was a bad idea, completely insane, she lifted her chin and brushed her lips over his. The light touch of the kiss made her shiver. "Now that would be tragic."

He cupped her face in his palm. "You have to help me, Grace. Only you can save me."

She sighed dramatically. "Well, if I must..." she said, and pressed her mouth to his.

Their playful kisses quickly turned heated, and she keened softly when he wrapped his arms around her waist and pulled her closer.

He growled in response, a low hum deep in the back of his throat, and parted her lips with his tongue. Her knees went weak when she tasted him, her toes curling in her sensible sandals. His kiss resonated in every fiber of her body, slow and deep, his tongue stroking hers. The taste of him was dark and sweet, and even as she let him go deeper, take more, she knew she'd made a mistake even starting this because she never wanted him to stop.

They parted for a breath, and he looked down into her eyes, smoothing the hair off her face. "This probably isn't a good idea."

He was right of course, but that didn't mean she was in any mood to listen to reason. "It's probably a very bad idea indeed."

Contrary to her words, she moved even closer to him, her breasts pressed hard against his chest.

She felt his sharp intake of breath, saw the desire darken his eyes. "Definitely morally objectionable. You are my client after all."

She giggled. She couldn't help it. She never knew how much fun it was to be wanton. "Good thing you're not a nice guy then."

He pulled her roughly against him. "You're absolutely right."

He kissed her again, hard and long and deep. She was tangled up in him, her body melded to his. Hunger overtook her sense, and she clung to him while he ravaged her mouth. She was swept up, carried away, and she let him guide her backwards to wherever he wanted to take her. He bit down on her lower lip and lifted her, sitting her down on top of the table that was suddenly behind her. Without thought, ruled by pure, animal need, she wrapped her legs around his waist and pulled him in. She gasped into his kiss when their bodies met, desire pulsing between her legs.

His hands immediately went to her thighs, rough and urgent, pushing her dress up. Her mouth fell away from his when he grabbed her, tugging her closer. His lips were on her throat, kissing and licking her sensitive skin. For now, right here, she wanted to forget who she was, forget every responsibility, every panic-inducing dilemma, and simply be with him. She grabbed his ass and pulled him in, the heat of him pressing into where she needed him most. Her thighs relaxed and let him in a little more. With a strangled cry, she bit down on his shoulder when he rocked against her.

He tore his mouth from her throat, took her hand, and brought it down to the bulge in his jeans. He was hot against her palm, hard and throbbing. She didn't care where she was, didn't care about what she was supposed to be doing, didn't care about rules or decorum or her own hang-ups. For once in her life, all she cared about was the moment. She ached for him, and all that mattered was that she wanted him as much as he wanted her. She reached for his belt and fumbled with the buckle.

His hands came off her, hovering in the air over her as she pushed the belt aside and curled her fingers around the top button of his jeans. She saw raw lust in his dark eyes, felt it pumping hot through her own veins. She held his gaze and unbuttoned the second button. Tension electrified the air, and she was very aware of the sound of her own panting breath, the heat in her core. One more button, and he was all hers.

"Hello?" a voice she recognized as Kat's called out, coupled with a knock on the door.

For one incredible second, all time stopped, and they were completely frozen. They looked at one another, and Grace had to fight back a wild urge to laugh.

"Yeah, Kat. Just a second," Ryan called back, hastily buttoning up his jeans.

She leapt to her feet, pulled her dress straight, and quickly ran her fingers through her hair. It was all so insane giggles erupted out of her, and she slapped her hand over her mouth to keep herself quiet. He grinned back at her and then asked if she was ready with a single raised eyebrow. She smoothed her hair one more time and nodded.

"Okay," he whispered and then opened the door.

Kat stood on the threshold. Her gaze went from Grace, to Ryan, and then back to Grace again.

She knows, Grace thought, and bit down on her lower lip.

Kat stepped inside, amusement playing on her lips. She focused on Grace. "I heard you were here, and I wanted to stop by and say hi. See what you thought of the site."

Grace smiled brightly. "I love it. Thank you so much."

"I'm glad." She gave them each a searching look. "We like to keep our clients...satisfied."

Grace's cheeks went scarlet, and she chewed on her tongue to keep from laughing. "I think I'll very satisfied."

Kat's smile only got wider. Her gaze flicked to Ryan and then back to Grace. "Yes, I can see how you would be."

"The site is beautiful," Grace answered, unable to think of anything else to say.

"Well," Kat said, spinning on her very high heel. "I need to get back to work myself. Will I see you at Ryan's fight on Friday?"

Grace nodded. "I'll be there."

"Great," Kat said, and headed for the door. Ryan held it open for her. "Oh, and Ryan?" Kat spoke softly, but Grace could still hear her. "Your belt's unbuckled." She looked back over her shoulder at Grace, gave her a wink, and then left the room.

Grace let herself laugh as Ryan scrambled to buckle his belt. She shook her head and leaned back against the table. "That was totally inappropriate."

He smiled. "Yes, it was. We should do it again immediately."

He reached for her, but her cell phone rang, shrill and insistent. She fumbled through her bag for it, and her heart stopped when she saw the caller ID.

"Hello?" she answered.

"Ms. Betancourt?" that cool, professional voice she hated so much asked.

"Yes?" Grace asked, dread and fear making her heart thud.

"Ms. Betancourt, this is Andrea Wilcox. I'm afraid your father's taken a bit of a tumble and accidently hit his head. He's being taken to Brookhaven Hospital now."

All the air went out of her lungs. "How bad?"

"He's going to require some stitches, and they will admit him for the night to make sure he isn't suffering from any other injuries. The doctor on duty will give you the full picture when you arrive at the hospital."

"Thank you." Her lips were numb. Everything was numb. "I'll be there shortly." She took the phone away from her ear and pressed the end button.

"Grace, what's wrong?" Ryan asked, standing close by her side. She hadn't even realized he was beside her.

She roused herself enough to look over at him. "I have to go."

She pushed herself off the table and brushed by him, heading for the exit. He grabbed her elbow before she could make it to the door.

"Grace," he said, gripping her biceps, forcing her to meet his gaze. "What's wrong?"

The command in his voice make her blink, forced her back to the present. "I have to go. My dad." She shook her head. Too many thoughts. "I have to get to the hospital."

His grip tightened on her. "What hospital?"

She was seeing everything through a daze. "Brookhaven. On Long Island."

"Okay," he said. "Sit down." He guided her to a chair. "I'll get you to Long Island."

"No," she said, popping back up. "I have to leave *now*."

"I understand." His voice was calm, soothing. He gently pushed her back into the chair. "Let me arrange a few things." He pulled his phone out of his pocket and made a call. "Jodi, this is Ryan. Please arrange for me to have a car." He paused, his hand never leaving her shoulder. "I need it now." Pause. "Thanks." He hung up and looked back at Grace. "Just one more call and we're good to go."

She shook her head. "You don't have to do this. I can get there fine."

"I know," he said. "I want to." He stood by her side, gently stroking her back while he made another call. He seemed to wait longer this time before finally speaking. "Dean, this is Ryan. I'm going to have to miss our meeting today. Something's come up. An emergency. Sorry. I'll catch up with you tomorrow." He ended the call and jammed the phone into his back pocket. "Okay, let's go."

"No," she said, taking her arm from his grasp. "Really, Ryan. I need…" What did she need? She wasn't sure.

"Grace," he said, patiently. "You're shaking. Let me just take you there, okay?"

She hadn't realized she was shaking. When did that happen? He put his arm around her and escorted her out of the room. They paused at the receptionist desk and the woman handed him a slip. "Thanks, Jodi," he said and looked at the paper. He led Grace outside. "We're going to a garage on West Broadway. Two blocks."

"Stop," she said, halting in the middle of the sidewalk, forcing tourists to dodge around her. Now that she was out in the fresh air, she had herself a bit more under control. "Look, I can do this on my own. Thanks, but you really don't need to come with me." She rubbed her hands over her face. "Let me arrange a car, and I can go."

He planted his feet and put his hands on his hips. "I'm not letting you drive out to Long Island alone. There's nothing you can say to change that."

Her mouth opened, then closed. He was not going to take no for an answer. He was making it so much more complex than it needed to be. Arguing was only going to delay things though. "Fine," she said, waving him forward. "Go."

They arrived at the garage, and Ryan handed the attendant the paperwork. The man took off into the rows of cars. He returned a moment later with a black, American sedan. The attendant held the passenger door open for Grace, saw her safely inside, and then shut the door. He jogged around the car to give Ryan the keys. Ryan handed him a folded bill in return. Grace couldn't see how much.

Ryan climbed into the driver's seat, and Grace looked out the window while he programmed the GPS unit with their destination.

Hopeless, that was how she felt. Useless.

"Tell me what happened," Ryan said as he pulled out into traffic.

She shook her head. "I don't even know where to start."

He glanced over at her, took her hand, and placed it on his thigh. "Start wherever you'd like."

His body was warm beneath her fingertips. It felt nice, but she hurt too much to truly care. "Five years ago, my father was diagnosed with Alzheimer's Disease. After my mother died, he got worse really quickly. I didn't have the skills or the space to care for him, so I did some research and found Westview Gardens, supposedly the best long-term care facility in the country for people with dementia. I called in every favor, pulled strings, found loopholes, did whatever I could to get him in there." She let out a tired breath. "Of course, it's not covered by insurance."

Ryan merged onto the Belt Parkway, quietly driving as she told her tale.

"He was doing well." Was he? "Or at least he was comfortable. I had hope." She tapped the window. "But this is the second time he's fallen down in as many weeks." She swallowed hard. "They say he's getting worse." The truth she didn't want to admit to herself. "That his motor skills are deteriorating." The sad, hard truth. "Today he fell down badly enough to require stitches. Maybe more."

"He's in the best possible care, Grace," Ryan said. "They will do everything they can for him."

"That's what everyone keeps telling me." All she could imagine was broken bones, fractured skull, internal bleeding.

"You're making yourself crazy. I can see it from here."

She knew he was right, but she couldn't stop. Not until she knew for sure what had happened to him. She took her hand off his leg and curled into herself, leaning her head against the passenger window. Traffic was light and they zipped toward the hospital in the carpool lane, passing couples and commuters, business people and families.

"How far away are we from where you write about?" he asked.

Grace watched the exits fly by. "About an hour. The pond is almost at the end of the island."

"I bet it's beautiful."

"It is," Grace agreed. "Very ritzy. A little quieter than the Hamptons people usually think of. Not so party orientated."

"Have you spent much time there?"

"No, it's funny actually. When I first moved to New York, I decided I wanted to try to find the Amityville Horror house."

He laughed, glanced at her, and then back at the road. "Why doesn't that surprise me?"

She smiled over at him. "Yeah." She paused. This was not a time for smiling. "Anyway, I rented a car and drove out here. I spent hours searching for 112 Ocean Avenue."

He raised an eyebrow. "You didn't find it?"

"No. Though I know it exists. It's a real place, you know?" She shook her head. "This was a while ago now, so phones didn't have GPS at the time, and the car didn't have a unit. I couldn't locate it at all." She looked out the car window, touched her fingers to the glass. "I didn't want to go back to the city right away, so I decided to do some driving, some exploring. I'd never been to Long Island before."

She let out a long breath. God, that was such a different time. Her mom was still alive, her dad healthy. So much could change in such a short while.

A gentle caress on her arm caught her attention, and she looked over at Ryan. "And that's how you found it?"

She narrowed her eyes at him even as her lips curved. "Are you trying to distract me?"

"Is it working?"

"Kinda."

He flashed her a quick grin. "Good. Tell me how you found the spot."

"Amityville was a bust, so I kept driving until I got hungry. I got off the highway at Wainscott. I found a cute café right on the

70

pond. It spoke to me. I loved it every bit of it. It was November, so there were no tourists or summer people around. It was quiet and pretty, very picturesque. I got a hotel room for the night and spent the next day walking around. I just knew it was the place."

"Did you always write?"

"I started out as a freelance journalist when I moved to New York, women's magazines mostly, the Sunday supplement in the paper, but I always wanted to write novels."

"Take Exit 54 in one point two miles," the GPS said.

"Almost there," she said, the weight in her chest alive again.

He glanced over at her once more, tenderly touched his knuckles to her cheek. "I'm here for you, Grace."

She did not want to feel what she was feeling for him. It was too much for one day. She took his hand and gave it a squeeze. "Thanks."

They followed the directions and found the hospital without incident. Ryan pulled into the first available parking spot and killed the engine. The ticking engine was very loud.

Grace took a deep breath, her eyes fixed on the entrance. What would she find beyond those glass doors? Nothing good. She didn't know if she could show the naked emotion she was probably going to face. It was probably something best done alone. She turned to Ryan. "Thank you for bringing me out here." Her gaze went back to the entrance. "I'll probably be awhile. You don't have to wait. You can go back to the city."

Ryan laughed, but not with any humor. "You're not getting rid of me now, Grace." He rested his wrist on top of the steering wheel and leaned over toward her. "Besides, how would you get home?"

She didn't want him to go, but she needed to face this alone. "There are trains to Penn Station."

"Please," Ryan said, opening the driver's door. "I'm not letting you take the train back to the city." He got out of the car, circled around the passenger's side, and opened the door. He held out his hand to her. "I can wait as long as you need me to."

She took his hand and let him help her out of the car. Maybe it wouldn't be so bad to have him around. She was very deeply frightened, but she had to admit, he gave her some strength. She looked toward the entrance again and willed herself to move forward. He took her hand, and they walked across the parking lot together.

The automatic doors parted and cool air touched her skin when they entered the lobby. An older woman was sitting at the information desk, a large security guard sitting beside her.

"The Yankees are going nowhere this year," the woman said as Grace approached. "Downright depressing. The Boss would've done something about it. God rest his soul."

"Excuse me," Grace said, her hands on the desk. "I'm looking for a patient?"

"Sure," the woman said, adjusting her glasses. "What's the name?"

"Roland Betancourt."

She typed the information into her computer, then pointed toward the elevator bank. "Take the green elevators to the fifth floor. When you exit, make a left. He's in room 502."

"Thank you," Grace said, sickening butterflies churning in her stomach.

Before she could walk away, Ryan leaned over the desk. "The Phillies are going to take it all this year. Just sayin'."

The woman cawed with laughter. She looked to Grace. "Your young man is mentally unstable. He needs professional help."

Your young man. She liked the way that sounded. It may not be the actual truth, but it was a nice thought. Grace cracked a smile. She couldn't help herself. "I think he's beyond help."

The guard shook his head sadly. "Poor boy probably thinks the Eagles have a chance too. Such a shame."

Ryan grinned. "This is Long Island, isn't it? Shouldn't you guys be Mets fans?"

The woman affected a scowl and pointed toward the elevators.

"Get away from my desk."

They left the staff smiling and went for the elevators. Grace's stomach flipped and plummeted. The hard truth was waiting up there. Ryan took her hand as the elevator door closed. She threaded her fingers through his, grateful for his support and for his stubbornness. She was glad he was by her side. It was nice not to be alone for a change, nicer than she could have ever imagined.

They exited the elevator and turned left just as the woman told them, passing by a couch and coffee table, an overstuffed chair and a rack of magazines. They walked down a hallway lined with plaques and followed the directions toward the right room number.

They approached the door just as a woman in a white lab coat was leaving. She looked at them over her glasses. "Ms. Betancourt?"

"Yes," Grace said.

"I'm Dr. Armex. Your father has just been brought to his room. We are admitting him for the night. If I can have a few minutes of your time, I'd like to go over his case with you."

"Okay," Grace said, swallowing back her fear.

"Good," the doctor said. "We can talk in my office." She looked from Grace to Ryan. "Is this your husband?"

"No," Grace said. "He's…" He's what? "My friend."

Dr. Armex nodded. "I can only discuss details with immediate family members."

"It's okay," Ryan said. "I'll be waiting for you back at the couch we passed."

"Are you sure?" Grace asked.

"Of course."

"It could be a while."

"I love *People Magazine*."

She smiled gratefully. "Thank you."

The doctor headed down the hallway, and Grace gave Ryan one last look over her shoulder before following. Dr. Armex opened her office door and gestured for Grace to take a seat in one of the visitor's chairs. The doctor sat in her leather chair and folded her hands on top of the desk. She studied Grace intently for a moment before she spoke.

"As I'm sure the people at Westview have explained to you, your father's motor skills are deteriorating. This fall will not be his last. The time is coming when he will need to be confined to a wheelchair."

Grace's heart sank. This was worse than she imagined.

The doctor leaned forward. "Don't lose hope, Ms. Betancourt. He is in very good hands. And we will do our best to make him as comfortable as possible. But I do worry about you. Caregivers and family members often suffer from anxiety and depression. Do you have some sort of support system? I can recommend several groups and resources in the area if you're interested in connecting with others."

"No," Grace said. "Thank you. I'm fine."

"You don't have to deal with this alone, Ms. Betancourt."

"I'm not alone." It was an automatic response, just something to placate the doctor, but she couldn't help but think of Ryan when she said it.

Dr. Armex nodded. "Okay. But if you'd ever like to know more, please don't hesitate to call me."

Grace forced a smile onto her face. "Thank you. I'd like to see him now if I could."

"Of course," the doctor said. "Do you remember where his room is located?"

"I do."

She stood and shook the doctor's hand. She stepped out of the office and made her way back down the hallway to her father's side.

Chapter Six

The sight of her dad sleeping in the hospital bed with all those bandages on his head made her physically ill. Tubes came out from every part of him, bags of things running into him, monitors beeping off his vital stats. She wanted to sob, to break down and curl into a little ball by his side and cry and cry and cry, but she promised herself she would never cry in front of him, and she wasn't about to break that promise now. He needed her to be optimistic, to believe in him. She dragged a guest chair over to the side of the bed, the rough cloth seat chafing her thighs as she tried to get somewhat comfortable.

"Hi, Dad," she said and took his withered hand. She looked down at his face and could not think of one thing to say. She had to blink hard and look up at the ceiling or the tears were going to spill down her face and she could not allow that. She gathered herself and tried again.

"You remember the website I told you about? Well, it came out great, and my web designer, his name is Ryan, is really nice. He's here now actually, out in the waiting area." A slight flush colored her cheeks as it often did when she thought of him, and she pushed the feelings aside. "You'd like him, I think. He's from Philly. He boxes. And he's really smart." 'Nice' and 'smart' sounded so lame. What else could she tell her dad though? That he was supremely hot? That he was a great kisser? That he had an amazing body?

Hell, no.

She licked her lips and looked back at her father. "We're still getting to know one another, but I think I might like him a lot." She smiled at her own foolishness, her own childish longing. But even her own happiness made her sad looking at her dad's still form. She stroked the back of his hand. "I really want you to meet him."

She lapsed into silence while the machines beeped and footsteps passed in the hallway. She could not think of a single thing more to say. If only there was something she could do to fix him, make him better. But there was nothing. She had to come to terms with the fact that he was never going to get better, that he was never going be able to meet Ryan in any real way.

She sat beside him for a long time, until her head started to hurt from holding back the tears. Her father slept on, oblivious to her anguish. For that, she was thankful. She was exhausted when she finally got up, kissed him goodbye, left the room.

Ryan was sitting on the couch just as he promised, reading a magazine. There was a woman sitting next to him, and an unshaved man. Ryan rose to his feet when she approached and took her hands in his. "Are you all right?"

"No." It was the only honest answer.

"What can I do?"

She shook her head. "Nothing."

"Come on, Grace," he said and put his arm around her shoulders. "Let me take you home."

They walked out to the parking lot. The night was dark and there were many stars. She looked up to see if she could locate the comet again, but it was nowhere to be found. Either the lights were too bright or it was gone.

Ryan opened the passenger door for her, and she got inside the car. The drive back to the city was uneventful and they passed it in silence. She was grateful for his quiet company. She was not in the mood for conversation.

He found a spot not far from her building and parked the car. He killed the engine and glanced over at her, concern in his eyes. "Can I walk you upstairs?"

Her gaze flicked toward her building, traveled up the façade to the windows of her dark apartment, the silence that awaited her there. She wasn't going to be able to get any writing done tonight. It was too early to go to sleep. She didn't want to watch a movie or read. She didn't even have a bottle of whiskey to see her through the long, lonely hours. If she sent him away, all she was going to do was sit on her couch and obsess. She didn't think she could bear to be alone with her own thoughts right now. She met his eyes and nodded.

The elevator was working, but they took the stairs instead, walking slowly up to the fifth floor. She let him in, flicked on the lights, and then locked the door behind them. "Do you want something to drink?"

"No," he said. "Do you want to talk about it?"

She opened her mouth. Closed it. It was still too fresh. She shook her head. "No."

He nodded slowly and opened his arms to her.

She didn't know how a simple hug could be her total undoing, but when she stepped into his arms, something released within her and all the stress, all the sadness and fear, broke, and the walls she had so painstakingly constructed around herself crumbled. His arms folded around her, enveloping her in warmth, and with a ragged breath, she gave herself over to his strength and cried.

"It's going to be okay, Grace," he murmured, gently stroking her hair.

It wasn't going to be okay, not in the slightest, but here, with him, in this one moment, it was. She closed her eyes, pressed her cheek against his chest, and let the steady beat of his heart soothe her tired soul. It was such a relief to be able to unload some of the devastating weight. Tears came to her eyes and instead of holding them back, she let herself cry in his arms. She wept for her dad, but for herself too, for all the stress and the grief and the sorrow. They stood in her living room, clinging to one another as the sobs wracked her chest. She let go in a way she never had before, and when her tears finally tapered off, she was bone-weary, but also cleansed.

She pushed back from him slightly. "Sorry," she mumbled. Embarrassment quickly replaced any comfort she might have felt, and she fumbled to wipe away the evidence of her momentary weakness. "I don't usually fall apart like that."

He just shook his head, then scooped her up into his arms. Her arms automatically wound around his neck, and she held on tight as he carried her down the hall. "You weren't kidding about that carrying thing, huh?"

He toed the bedroom door open and looked down into her eyes. "No, I wasn't."

He laid her down in her bed and then sat down by her feet. He lifted her legs onto his lap and began unbuckling her sandals.

"I'm not an invalid, Ryan." She didn't protest too hard though. She was liking the treatment. No one had touched her this tenderly for a long time.

"I know." He placed her shoe on the floor and then started on her other foot. "When I was eight years old, my father left," he said, carefully working on the buckle. "Nothing dramatic or anything, just went off to work one day and never came back. My mother... She didn't take it that well. She kind of broke."

Grace listened in silence, watching the side of his face, his head bowed over her feet. Even though he didn't look at her, she felt the connection between them, the profoundness of the moment. This was probably something he never shared with anyone else—just like the tears she had cried earlier.

"The next day, she wouldn't get out of bed, didn't go to work. She wouldn't feed herself—wouldn't do anything—just laid there and cried. I got myself to school and all day long, I prayed that she would be back to normal when I got back home." He slipped the sandal off her foot, rested it beside the other one on her bedroom floor. "She wasn't."

He caressed the back of her calf, his touch light and warm. "By dinnertime, I understood that I had to take care of her. There was nothing else to do. She wouldn't function on her own. All I wanted to do was curl into her arms and cry too, but the time for that had long passed." He glanced up at her, gave her a tight smile, then bowed his head again. "I know what it's like to have to be strong all the time, Grace, to be the one that has to care for them, for everything to be backwards. I didn't have anyone to cry with back then, but, honey, you can cry with me anytime you'd like."

She had to swallow back the lump in her throat before she could speak. His fingers were a solid, steady weight on her legs, the warmth of his caress chasing away her doubts, her embarrassment. With him, she was stronger, with him she was better, and with him maybe she wouldn't have to be alone anymore, to shoulder the full weight of everything by herself. It was a scary thought, but one she might want to get accustomed to. She waited for him to meet her eyes, wishing once again that she could be as articulate in real life as she was in text. "Thank you."

He nodded. "I should probably get back to Brooklyn now."

His hands were warm on her bare legs, his touch tender. Everything about him was gentle when he was around her, when he held her, but that was only one side of him. She'd seen his posture change when he'd spotted the looters, saw the remnants of the black eye he had from fighting, the scarred knuckles. She could feel the strength in his grip. She needed some of that strength tonight. She didn't have any of her own left.

She reached out and traced the outline of his sideburn with her fingertip. The short, dark hair tickled the pad of her finger. Her heart raced as her gaze dropped to his lips, the decision bubbling in her core. "Do you have to leave right away?"

He shook his head slowly, his eyes never leaving hers. "No."

She leaned toward him, her gaze flicking from his eyes to his

79

mouth and then back again. He didn't move, remained perfectly still, letting her come to him. She touched his face, soft stubble against her palm. His scent filled her head; clean, sexy man. Her lips brushed over his, the contact igniting sizzling heat in her veins.

She felt him gasp when their lips met, a sharp inhalation that made her shiver. She pressed her lips to his, a closed-mouth kiss that sent tingles through every part of her. His fingers locked in her hair, and he cradled the back of her head as the kiss went on and on. They parted, then came back for more, his tongue tracing the seam of her lips, begging for entrance. When she finally opened for him, the electric shock of his tongue meeting hers made her quake.

He took the kiss deeper, and she moaned into him, melting into his strong arms. She snuggled closer to explore the broad expanse of his back, the lean muscle beneath his shirt. The man was a wall of sleek, solid muscle. Her body stirred ferociously in response to him, his touch, his scent. The need arose in her to taste his warm skin, explore all the dips and contours of his lithe frame, submit to all his strength, and for once in her life totally succumb to her desires. His hands moved over her, up and down her back, her waist, finally cupping her breast in one hand. Craving buzzed down her spine, heating her blood.

Their mouths met again and again, urgent, hungry. She reached under his shirt, his skin warm and smooth. She raked her fingernails over the small of his back and he bit down on her lower lip. He wrapped his arms around her waist and pulled her onto his lap. Every inch of him was pressed against her, and she was instantly and intimately aware that his chest wasn't the only part of him that was rock-hard and hot. She shivered when he caressed her breast through her dress, his thumb flicking her nipple until she groaned with need. Her fingernails dug into his shoulders, and she rocked against him, begging for more.

He broke the kiss with a ragged gasp and looked up into her eyes as he smoothed her hair off her face. "Are you sure you want to do this, Grace?" He ran his knuckles over her cheek. "We can wait."

She blinked and sat up, not liking this turn of conversation. "You want to wait?"

"No," he said with a laugh. "Definitely not." His face softened. "But maybe… Are you sure? Tonight?"

In that instant, Grace wanted him with a need so potent, it momentarily stunned her. She had never wanted any man this way. "Yes, Ryan. Tonight."

His full, sensual lips curved in a wicked grin. God, he was gorgeous. Simply stunning. "Well, you won't hear any argument from me."

When he leaned in for another kiss, she knew she'd made the right decision.

She lost herself in him, in his arms, in the gentle caress of his fingers on her spine. His muscles flexed under her hands, strong and sure and hard. He was by far the most powerful man she had ever been in bed with, and his strength was a little intimidating, but also wildly exciting. He kissed down to the hollow of her throat and gently licked there, his tongue teasing her hypersensitive skin. His hot breath on her neck sent a thousand chills along her nerve endings.

She traced his jaw, a feathery caress that made him moan softly. Her throat was dry, her body aching for him. She needed this tonight. She needed him tonight. She lifted his shirt off over his head and tossed it aside. His body was magnificent, every muscle defined, and she ran her fingers over his biceps, in awe of his beauty.

His hands moved up her thighs, taking her dress up with them, his fingertips resting at the edge of her panties. She gasped as he kissed her, the anticipation of his touch electrifying. She rocked against the heat of him, the hardness of him, encouraging him to go further. His hand moved up and up, taking the dress with him, lifting it off her. A low sound escaped his throat when he unhooked her bra and her breasts spilled out into his hands.

He looked up at her, his eyes dark in the dim room. "You are breathtaking."

She blushed, just like she always did, and he grinned. Before she could think, he flipped her over, and she laughed as she landed on her back on the bed. Nothing she had ever experienced compared to the arousing weight of him on her, the clean manly scent of him on her skin.

He smiled down at her and ran his fingers down the center of her body. Her chest heaved as she struggled for air. Anticipation pounded her chest. He nuzzled her throat, teasing the skin around her tummy with light caresses. His short nails scraped over her belly button and slowly, excruciatingly slowly, he dragged them down. Her muscles jumped and her hips bucked, silently willing him to go a little lower. His mischievous grin drove her wild. "Hmm," he hummed against her throat, the vibrations of his deep voice pulsating right down to her core. "Is there something you want, sweetheart?"

She laughed. She couldn't help herself. He was crazy. Her hand stroked down his chest, following the long line of soft, dark hair that bisected his amazing body. She lingered over his belt buckle, toying with the waistband of his jeans. "Yes," she said, looking up into his eyes. "There is something I want."

He sucked in a sharp breath when she gave him a gentle squeeze that was so erotically gratifying she couldn't help but gasp along with him. He was hot and hard in her hand, and huge, bigger than any man she had ever been with, and thought of him filling her was terrifyingly arousing. Oh yes, she wanted him *very* badly.

"There's something I want to do first," he said, his voice husky. His lips hovered over hers, his breath on her cheek. She was shaking from the force of her desire. He held her gaze as his hand glided down over her mound. "I want to taste you."

Her body went liquid when his hand moved between her thighs. She was slick, hot, needy. He kissed her hard, thrusting his tongue deep into her mouth. The kiss was long and deep, entwining and tangling, and she was so caught up in him, she didn't realize he'd slipped her panties off until the cool night air touched her hot, wet folds.

He slid a finger along the length of her entrance and her heart galloped into warp speed. She panted as he trailed kisses down her throat and over the valley of her breasts. The faint brush of his fingertips over her most intimate core set her pulse thudding and bands of ravenous pleasure pulsated through her being. She ground against him, needing more pressure, and placed her hand over his to show him what she wanted. She writhed while he teased her, giving her everything she had asked for and more, driving her into a feverish need.

She trembled from the tension, the craving, and she gasped when he moved down her body, parting her legs so that he could lie between them. His hot breath on her inner thigh set off a chain reaction of lust, and she had to press her lips together to keep from crying out from frustration and need. She moaned when his fingers gently opened her up, her wet desire aching for his touch. She was on the brink of screaming when he paused, met her gaze, and then dipped his head between her thighs.

"Oh my God." Her hips came up off the bed, the electric shock of his tongue sending bolts through her entire being.

Heat snaked up her spine, lighting her skin on fire. Her fingers sank into his thick hair and she moved with him, a slave to the pace that he set. He devoured her, savored her, his clever tongue taking her to heights she never dreamed attainable. Excited pulses echoed through her body, a rhythm of the most urgent need. She bit back a piercing scream, when his palms slid under her ass, dragging her closer to his mouth, lips, tongue.

She was completely at his mercy, and she surrendered to his touch, his inherent mastery. She writhed under him and he drove her crazy, making her pant from a pleasure that bordered on agony. His teeth nipped her flesh and goosebumps cascaded all over her skin. A strangled yelp escaped her lips when he pushed two fingers inside her, igniting sparks throughout her overloaded nervous system. Exquisite, unbearable need accompanied an intense rush of desire, and she gripped his hair harder. There was no way she could hold off even though she wanted to savor every lick and thrust. She had no control over her body's reaction, and she rode out the spasms that overtook her with a deafening cry.

He licked her even as she quaked, wringing out every last bit of pleasure. Her mind was blown, she thought she'd never be able to recover from the throbbing climax, and she had to push him away to make the agonizing pleasure end. It was simply too much. He kissed his way up her body, pausing to nuzzle her throat. His teeth clamped down on her neck, sending a shockwave of intense sensual pleasure all along her nerve endings. "I need a condom." His voice trembled. "Please."

For one scary second, she didn't think she had any. Oh please, God, she prayed as she rolled over in bed to open her nightstand drawer. She prayed some more as she riffled through the debris, tissues, pens, her vibrator. Ryan ran his hand down her back, took a fistful of her ass and gave it a nip. Oh no, she didn't want to miss out on him tonight. Just when she thought hope was lost, she found a strip of three in the back corner. She pulled them out and held them up triumphantly.

He took the packages from her and stood up to remove his jeans. His pants fell to the floor with a soft thump. He was all corded strength and naked beauty. His broad shoulders tapered down to a narrow waist, his abs a tight and honed six-pack, his thighs muscled and hard. His cock jutted out from a thick, dark thatch of wiry hair. Grace licked her lips, craving him to her very core. She watched, fascinated, as he ripped one of the condoms open and rolled it on. He caught her looking and gave her a smug grin before jumping playfully on top of her. She squealed with absolute delight and welcomed him into her arms.

He rested on his elbows above her and she looked up at him in total awe. He was so handsome, so sexy, and he wanted her. It was beyond comprehension. A surge of emotion overwhelmed her as he eased his body over hers and snuggled between her thighs. She stared into his eyes as he pushed inside, the pleasure overwhelming. She flexed beneath him, urging him in deeper. He kissed her face, her jaw, her mouth.

"I want you so much," he whispered, his voice raw against her lips.

The words pierced her soul, vibrating right down to the very core of her existence. She met his gaze, saw the desire, the truth in their dark depths. This was more than just sex, more than anything she had ever felt with another human being. Emotion, desire, passion overloaded her system and her heart swelled in her chest. This was the connection she had always secretly yearned for, but never believed could be real. She looked away, embarrassed by the intensity of the moment. This couldn't really be happening. She couldn't really be seeing what she thought she saw in his eyes. She was probably delusional—or perhaps just plain crazy.

He cupped her chin and brought her eyes back to his. "I feel it too."

She almost choked on the gasp that rose in her throat. She had never felt this way about anyone. He did crazy things to her. Crazy wonderful things. She pulled him closer, bringing him deeper inside her. A violent shudder racked her body, her muscles spasming around him, struggling to accommodate his unbelievable girth. Pain and pleasure met, merged and fed off one another, heightening her arousal. She moved her hips, wanting more, and he sunk in another incredible inch.

"Grace." He groaned. "Oh, God, you're so good."

He moaned and went in a little deeper. She was enveloped in him, in his arms, his scent, his strength. His mouth hovered over hers, his breath was her breath. She looked up and saw that his eyes were squeezed shut, his jaw clenched, and she could feel him trembling. He held his body rigid, as though he was holding back, and she wrapped her arms around his neck.

"Ryan, please," she gasped, needing him to end the erotic torture

85

and take her completely. Her sanity fled, leaving her aching, needy, intent on reaching the ultimate pleasure. She arched her hips, taking him deeper still, and she cried out his name when he pushed all the way inside.

The entire length of him plunged into her, and her chest heaved, her thighs convulsed. She felt so full. So complete. He pulled back and thrust into her again. She screamed, biting down on his shoulder. The pleasure was torturous. It was never this good for her. Ever.

He nuzzled her nose and licked her bottom lip. He stroked her cheeks with his thumbs and smiled down into her eyes. "Like that?"

She squealed with delight and wrapped her whole body around his. She gripped his hair in her fists and gave him a tug. He laughed and took her harder, deeper. His fingers dug into her flesh, his body rocking along with hers.

He braced himself over her, his palms resting on either side of her, denting the mattress. He dipped his head, his tongue thrusting into her mouth, making her gasp. He overtook every single one of her senses, and she moaned into his mouth, arching off the bed to kiss him harder. He plunged into her again and again, taking her to the place where love and lust melded and merged. Became one. Ecstasy exploded behind her closed eyes, and she stretched for it, reached for it, every cell in her body needing to get there.

He claimed her with every stroke, giving her more with every thrust, holding nothing back. "That's my girl," he whispered urgently. "Come hard for me, Grace. Come so hard for me…"

And with a sobbing cry, she did.

Above her, she faintly heard his hoarse shout and then he was groaning in her ear, a delightfully deep, throaty growl that made her hot all over again. He clung to her while he came, panting against her throat, his breath a hot caress all of its own. There was nothing on this earth like it and Grace thought she might do just about anything to feel it again, to hear him again, to be with him again.

He fell back on the bed and they lay sprawled beside one another, spent and sated. She could hear his ragged breath and knew she was panting loudly as well. Her body was still shuddering from the aftershocks of her pleasure and she smiled up at the ceiling, completely at peace.

Ryan rolled onto his side and took her into his arms. She snuggled against him, glowing from a sense of utter contentment. His hard body stretched out beside her, warm and firm. She traced patterns on his skin, exploring the contours of his muscles.

"How did you get this?" she asked, her fingers tracing the scar above his right eyebrow.

"Boxing. It was my second fight ever, back in Philly. A left-hander. He caught me by surprise. I got hit hard."

"And this?" she asked, stroking the faded scar on his collarbone.

"I got that when I was fourteen, playing lacrosse. I got body checked by this huge guy on the other team. He took me down, and I landed right on my shoulder."

She winced, lightly caressing his skin. "Ouch."

He smiled, his hands running slowly up and down her back, sketching patterns along her spine. "Yeah."

"People like to abuse you, huh?" It was so nice to lay here with him and explore his body. His beautiful body.

He laughed. "I deserve it most times." His hand moved to her forearm. "Looks like you've got one of your own. What's this from?"

"I fell out of a tree when I was ten. I wanted to rescue a cat that climbed up it." She moved closer to him, emotion closing her throat. "My dad used to be the fire chief. I wanted to be just like him. I thought he was the biggest, strongest man in the world."

His thumb brushed over her cheek. "They're going to do whatever they can to help him."

"I know," she said softly. "It's just that there isn't all that much help for him anymore."

He looked down into her eyes. "No matter what, you *will* get through this. I'm here for you."

Moisture pricked the back of her eyeballs, but she willed it away. She could not deal with any more crying tonight—not even the good kind. "Thanks."

He nuzzled her temple. "We'll go back tomorrow and check on him."

"Ryan…" She couldn't see him tomorrow. She had to work. She'd go see her dad alone later in the day. Being with Ryan would mean way too much distraction. And an afternoon trip with him would probably turn into a whole night together. It was temping, *very tempting*, but she had other responsibilities. It was imperative that she meet every one of her deadlines. "I can't go with you tomorrow. I'm busy. Booked. I have to write."

He frowned. "Grace, I don't know where you think this is going, but I want to see you more than once a week."

She ran her fingertips over the muscles in his arms. It was hard not to feel safe in arms like these. She wanted to be with him, but her career came first. Making money had to come first. "Ryan, if you want this to work, I'm going to need space. Time to write. I want to be with you, but it can't be every day. It can never be every day."

"I understand," he said, drawing her closer. "We'll work it out. But this week, I get you not only Friday night for the fight, but all day Saturday too." He kissed her. "And that means Saturday night as well."

Everything in her cringed. This was exactly why she'd been staying away from relationships. People needed attention. Required it. He was asking her to give up a whole two days of writing, days that were now more important than ever. But she wanted to be with him. She'd never felt anything like the comfort she felt in his arms. Didn't she deserve some happiness? One little thing all for herself? She recalled the way he'd looked at her when they made love. There had been something real there. Something special. A connection she did not want to deny. If she wanted him, then she needed to double down, work harder, rearrange her word count goals. It was going to be difficult, she was already almost stretched to her limits, but she thought she could do it. She had to. It was the only way to have it all. She would make it work, even if it meant she never slept again. "Okay," she said and kissed his lips. "And all day Saturday too."

Chapter Seven

Ryan heard the sounds of voices and music outside the locker room, but they were distant, unimportant. His own fight wasn't scheduled to begin for another half an hour, and he sat on the hard wood bench, staring at the blank wall, surrounded by the line of metal lockers. Other men moved around him, showering, dressing, preparing for their fights, but Ryan paid them no attention. He was lost in thoughts of Grace.

When he'd woken up in her bed on Wednesday, he'd never been a happier man. He'd reached for her instantly, her skin soft and warm, her body yielding to his touch. They'd made long slow love in the early morning light, the kind of love he had never quite experienced before. There was no urgency, no rush to fulfill a primal, physical need. It was a slow, intimate exploration, one which took him to realms of pleasure he never thought possible.

Sleeping with his first client was probably the worst choice he'd ever made. It was probably going to get him fired. At the very least, it was unethical.

He didn't regret it one bit.

If anything, he'd wanted more. He'd wanted to shower with her, linger, make love again, stay in bed with her all day long, but she was firm in her desire for him to go, and he did have to get to work. He didn't often play hooky, but if she had been willing to let him stay, he would've called in sick without a second thought. He didn't press the issue, there was a lot waiting for him at the office. Among a million other things, he'd missed his meetings with Dean and Ron when he'd taken her to Long Island, and he needed to reschedule those. So, he'd left with a kiss and a promise to see each other at the fight. He'd thought about her every day since that morning, her soft moans and gasps, the scent of her skin, the sound of her laughter, the way her lips curved when she smiled, the rosy blush that so often colored her cheeks. Every bit of him ached to see her again, and he'd spent a long and lonely few days without her.

He'd texted her since then, checking in on her and her dad, but it wasn't enough. He needed to see her. Touch her. He missed her. He'd never felt this way about anyone before, and he had to admit, he liked it. A lot.

A loud cheer erupted from outside the locker room, and he looked toward the exit. He wondered if Grace had arrived yet. He'd left a ticket for her just as he'd promised at the box office. The thought of her in the audience while he fought made his stomach flutter with nervous anticipation. He wanted to win while she watched, while she was cheering for him. And then they could celebrate his victory in style, and not leave his bed for twenty-four whole hours—or more if he could convince her to stay.

He blinked and smiled, his own thoughts surprising him not only with their clarity, but also with the warm contentment that gathered in his chest. These were not things he ever thought he wanted. He wanted to be carefree, not tied down, not an emotional slave to the whims of others. "I want you," he'd told her. They were words he'd spoken in past, but those words were so often empty, a pretty lie to get what he wanted. All that changed when he held Grace in his arms.

His coach, Miles Michener, entered the room and gave Ryan a mighty frown. Miles was always frowning. He was probably about sixty years old, grizzled, jaded, demanding, and the best trainer

Ryan had ever had the pleasurable misfortune to work with. It was because of Miles he'd made it as far as he did. Not that that pleased the man. Not in the least. He analyzed the tapes of every fight, went over Ryan's mistakes in excruciating detail, and pushed him to do better. He crossed the room and stood over Ryan, his arms folded across his chest.

"You ready?"

Ryan met the man's faded blue eyes and nodded. "Yeah."

Miles's frown deepened the laugh lines on his face as he took Ryan's hands to double-check the wraps, making sure everything was in order. "Your girl's here."

Ryan blinked. He'd expected Miles to chastise him for something or another, not this random non sequitur. "My girl?"

Miles held up one glove for Ryan to slip on. "Yeah, your girl. The one you left the ticket for. She's here."

"That's good." He grinned like an idiot as he pushed his hand into the glove. His girl. Grace. He liked the sound of that an awful lot.

"I take it this one's going to be around more than a day or two?"

Ryan's eyebrows shot up. "What're you talking about?"

"Kid, you've slept with every girl on the circuit, and you've only been around for about six months. If I'd never seen you in the ring, I'd think you had no discipline at all."

His coach's comment stung more than Ryan cared to admit. "I have discipline."

"Why do you box?" he asked, sliding the second glove onto Ryan's hand.

Ryan shifted on the bench, not liking the turn in conversation. He doubted he'd ever be comfortable when asked for an honestly emotional response, so, as usual, he shrugged it off with a quick grin. "'Cause it's fun."

Miles grunted. "Save the bullshit for someone else, all right?"

"Because it's the one anchor in my life." The admission was the raw, brutal truth, and it left him naked.

If Miles heard the thickness in Ryan's voice, he chose to ignore it. "Anchors are good, but it's not something you can take for granted. It's something you gotta build, you get me? You can have one, big, stupendous punch that makes the crowd go, 'Ooo,' without any training, but it means nothing if you can't stick around for the entire match." He held Ryan's gaze. "And to have the endurance to do that, means putting in an effort every single day."

Effort. Endurance. Sticking around. He wanted those things to apply to himself, to his life—mostly especially to his new life with Grace. He nodded, taking the words to heart. "I get you."

"Good." The older man laced the glove up tight. "Now, are you going to win or are you gonna go out there and look like a damn fool in front of her?"

Ryan couldn't help but smile. "I'm going to win."

Miles eyed him closely. "You aren't all that good-looking to begin with, Granger. Don't take it in the face like you did last time, okay?"

He winced at the memory. "I'm going to try and avoid that."

Miles strapped the headgear securely under Ryan's chin. "You do that. A girl that pretty doesn't want an ugly guy at her side."

He couldn't argue with that. "You're probably right."

Miles glanced at the clock mounted over the lockers. "It's time."

Ryan stood up, exhaled a hard breath.

"Whose ring is this?" Miles asked.

The blood surged in Ryan's veins, the feral desire to compete and win. "Mine."

"Damn right it is." Miles put his hands on Ryan's shoulders and looked directly into his eyes. "You got this."

He did have it. This fight was his. He walked out of the locker room.

He entered the event area and gaped at the size of the crowd. Every chair was taken and people milled about around the side-lines. He spotted Kat and Dean down in the third row, and next to them, Ron and Alan. There were other various people from the office and their dates scattered around. He looked everywhere as he made his way to the ring, searching for her in the sea of faces. Anxiety jangled his nerves, setting his teeth on edge. Miles said she was here. Why couldn't he find her?

And then he saw her, standing close by his corner. She had a red dress on and her hair was piled high on her head. She was the loveliest thing he had ever seen.

"Grace," he said, but the word was lost in the noise. She must have sensed the weight of his stare though, because she looked up at that moment and caught his eye. When she smiled, all was right in his world.

He climbed into the ring and took his corner. There was a bigger crowd then he expected, and it was louder than he had ever heard it in a gym. Anticipation flooded his senses, the rush of the fight to come, and he wanted to lash out, punch hard, strike quick and fierce, really tear into his opponent, but he breathed deep, filling his head with the familiar scents of sweat and disinfectant, chlorine from the pool, to keep himself centered. Getting all revved up like that was a recipe for disaster. Boxing required focus, skill. He wasn't some street brawler. He was a fighter.

He looked at his opponent across the ring, another middle-weight he'd never met before. But then, Ryan didn't know many people. He was still too new to the New York scene. The man was built very much like he was, a little over six-feet tall, broad shoulders, probably around one-eighty. Ryan wasn't worried. This match was his.

The host introduced the fighters, and Ryan waved as his friends cheered for him. It sounded like he had quite a support group out there. It was a damn good feeling. His gaze went to Grace for a brief instant, and when she looked back at him, he knew he would win this fight for her.

The bell rang, signaling the start of the first round, and Ryan circled his opponent. He swung and connected, satisfied by the way the man's head snapped back. The first point was his. The goal in this tournament wasn't a knockout or a big sucker punch, but to be technically accurate and land solid, regulation punches. A little bit of blood didn't hurt though.

Ryan connected with another punch to his opponent's head. Another solid point. Three minutes was not a long time when sitting at a desk, but in the ring, it was ages. He couldn't avoid the man's fists the whole time and gave up a few hits. Still, when the bell rang, he was ahead.

Round two began and it started out as more of the same, promising to be another grueling three minutes of total concentration. He hit the man hard wherever he could, hoping to wear him down. He concentrated on his jabs, snapping them out with speed and precision, but in the process dropped his right guard. His opponent took advantage and tagged Ryan with a devastating hook on the chin. It wasn't a knockout shot, but it was close. Clean and powerful, it was hard enough to rock him back on his heels and leave his head buzzing. The only thing that kept him on his feet was the horrifying thought of Grace watching him fall. He'd lost many fights in the past, but he couldn't bear to fail in front of her. He found her in the crowd, standing in his corner, and her smile helped him gather enough of his wits to dance away from his opponent's fists. He wasn't clear headed enough to fight back, but she gave him the strength to stay upright until the bell finally saved him.

"Are you going easy on him? Is that your plan? Cause it's working," Miles said when Ryan returned to his corner.

His head was still ringing, and he blinked his eyes, willing them to focus. "I'm just wearing him down."

"Well, cut it out and box," Miles commanded.

"Yeah," Ryan replied dryly. "I'm getting right on that."

The bell for the third round sounded, and Ryan was ready. He circled the other man, wary of that nasty hook. He was not going to get tagged again if he could help it. That last hit had put him behind, and he needed to take some more shots, get in a few more decent punches before it was over. He threw out a few jabs to keep his opponent off balance, forcing him to defend instead of attack. He kept the pressure on, hoping to get the opportunity for a real shot, a solid right or a hook to the body, whatever he could get to score some points

He caught a lucky break, jabbing his opponent in the solar plexus, and Ryan smiled as the air whooshed out of the other man's lungs. He followed it up with a tight upper cut that sent his head flying back. Two more points right there. He feigned right, then skipped out of the man's range before he could recover and retaliate.

He didn't know how much longer he had, but he knew it was going to end soon. This was the best part of fighting for him, those last few minutes where he was not only tested by his opponent, but also by the strength of his will and the stamina of his body. Could he stay on his feet? Could he endure? Sometimes that answer was no. He hoped that would not be the case tonight.

He swung again, but only caught air. He was really sweating now, working hard just to stay steady. He went for another point, something quick and easy, but the bell rang, ending the fight.

Ryan held his breath while the judges tallied the points. It was a close match. The winner was announced over the loudspeaker, and he cheered inwardly right along with the audience when his name was called. He wanted to jump up and down, scream and snarl, but that would come later. Gloating was bad form and just plain rude. He allowed the ref to hold his hand up high over his head, and he grinned wildly at the crowd. He couldn't wait to see Grace and celebrate in style.

People swarmed around him as he cleared the ropes, but there was only one person he wanted to see. He spotted her toward the back of the well-wishers, waiting patiently for him to get to her. He cut through the throng, his eyes focused on his one and only goal.

"YAY!" she screamed when he got close and opened her arms up wide.

He swept her up in gigantic hug. This was the best win ever. Not only was he the champion, but he had this amazing woman to share it with. He was lucky beyond all his dreams. He swung her around just because he could and because she felt so damn good in his arms. They were going to make love so hard tonight.

He set her back down on her feet and gave her a tremendous kiss. He wanted to share every moment of his life with her, joy like this, but the hard stuff too, like helping her with her father. He never wanted to be without her. Being with her was everything to him and he was totally in love with her.

He jerked back from her, the truth hitting him harder than the man in the ring ever could. Love? Really? Is this what it felt like?

"Congratulations," she said, grinning up at him.

He looked at Grace, into her beautiful face, the face he wanted to wake up to every morning of his life. He was in love with her. Totally, madly, completely in love with her. There was no other name for what he felt, no other explanation for the passion thumping in his chest. It was unlike anything he had ever felt before or even imagined possible. No wonder his mother chased after it, succumbed to it again and again. For the first time in his life, he understood.

"Um, Ryan?" a female voice asked, accompanied by a tap on his shoulder.

The voice was vaguely familiar, and he turned toward the sound, curious, but also a bit annoyed by the intrusion. Couldn't this person see he was busy? Whoever it was, he intended to get rid of them quickly, but when he caught sight of the blonde woman standing behind him, his eyes bugged out of his head. It was the Ring Card Girl from the last fight.

"Hi, ahhh…" Fuck! He still didn't know her name.

The woman looked at Grace and cocked her head to the side. "Who's this?"

"Ryan?" Grace asked from beside him. "What's going on?"

Wait, no, this was not right. Something was wrong here. Why was this woman here? He looked from one to the other, catching the dangerous vibe flowing between them. He was in trouble. Lots of trouble. He needed to say something, do something to diffuse this situation, but his mouth only hung stupidly open, no words coming out.

The Ring Card Girl's eyes narrowed. "I'm Willow," she said to Grace. "Did he invite you here are well?"

Grace's eyes got big when she looked at him. "You invited her?"

"Grace, I can explain," he began. How in the hell was he going to explain this? Had he invited the other woman? He must have. There was no other reason for her to be there.

"Oh, you can explain it to *her*?" Willow asked. She looked from him, to Grace, back to him. "I see." She gave him a hard look, bitter and angry. "He must have forgotten to tell you that he invited me as well."

Grace's lips pursed, as though she had tasted something sour. "Did you seriously forget inviting her?"

"Ah…" He shook his head, silently pleading with Grace. "I'm sorry." Shit! What could he say? "It didn't mean anything."

"It didn't mean anything?" Willow flamed. "It doesn't mean anything to you when you sleep with someone and then invite them somewhere?"

Grace's mouth fell open. "You *slept with her* and you forgot?" She shook her head, dumbfounded. "You slept with her, and it didn't mean anything? Really, Ryan?"

The woman smirked. "I'm guessing he slept with you too then, huh? Did he tell you how much he wanted you? Whisper it in your ear?"

His lungs seized up, strangling him. This was not the way it was supposed to go. Her words made a mockery of everything he felt for Grace. It hadn't been the same at all. He looked to his love, needing to explain himself, needing her to understand. "Grace—"

She held up her hand, halting whatever he was going to say, her clear disappointment and hurt—God, help him there was so much hurt on her face—shattering his soul. She didn't know it was different, didn't realize that though his words may have been the same, the sentiment was absolutely not. Her misunderstanding of everything that happened between them destroyed him. He hated himself.

"You are not the man I thought you were," she said, the misery in her eyes drilling into the depths of his being. "You're a pig."

A sledgehammer of pain smashed into his heart, nearly bringing him to his knees. "No, Grace, please—"

Disgust twisted her beautiful features. "Ryan, there's nothing you can say here that is going to make this better." She looked to the other woman. "I'm sorry. I didn't know."

Willow shook her head. "Don't apologize to me. You're not the asshole."

Grace nodded to the woman, looked back to him. "Goodbye, Ryan."

"No, Grace!" He reached for her, but she evaded his grasp. He went after her, but people surrounded him, groping and hugging him, offering their smiles and congratulations. Grace slipped away through the crowd, toward the exit. Ryan watched her go, helpless to stop her.

Monday morning came far too quickly. Ryan dragged himself to the office, not at all ready to take on the day.

"Hey, Ryan," Jodi said when he entered. She blinked as she fully took him in. "Wow, you look pretty awful."

"Thanks," he said as sarcastically as possible. He had not had a very good weekend. No sleep. No food. All he could think about was Grace and how he was going to get her back.

"Well, I hate to add to your already obviously bad day, but 'Mrs. Grinch' is looking for you."

Ryan groaned. He usually didn't mind dealing with Gwendolyn Pierce, he was one of the few people that could, but after the weekend he'd had, he was not in the mood to be ripped a new one today. The only reason she could be looking for him was to yell at him for something. "Any chance I can avoid her?" he asked Jodi.

The pretty receptionist shook her head, her multi-colored hair swinging from side to side. Today her blonde base was dipped in hues of pinks and purples. She gave him a sad face. "She seemed really tense. She's called twice. I'll think she'll hunt you down if you don't go see her."

He ground his teeth and gave into the despair. "I always did want a second asshole."

Jodi gave him a sympathetic look, but she was smiling. At least one woman smiled at him. He thought she might be the only one to do so today. "Sorry."

He did his best to smile back. "No worries. You're just the harbinger of bad news, that's all."

"I heard you won on Friday," she said, merrily changing the subject. "Sorry I missed it. Congratulations!"

"Thanks," he said. "It was a good fight." And a terrible night. He nodded toward the interior of the office. "I guess I should get going."

"See ya, Ryan."

"Yeah, later, Jodi."

He walked away from reception and headed toward his cubicle. He dropped his stuff on top of his desk and tried to decide what he wanted to do. He had two options. He could hide here and make Gwendolyn find him or he could go upstairs and face the music. If she called down and Jodi told her that he had been here for a while and not gone up to see her, the inevitable punishment would only be worse. He let out an aggrieved groan and headed for the staircase. Might as well get it done.

He trudged up the stairs, inwardly grumbling all the way. There was no telling what he'd done to incur her wrath this time, but he was sure it was something minor and silly. Gwen did like to blow things out of proportion. When he got to the top floor, he hesitated, looking over at Kat and Dean's alcove. Maybe he should poke his head in there and check in with his supervisor, see if there were any projects he could get in on. Or maybe talk to Kat about her latest comic, get a preview of the next episode. His body turned in that direction, but another finance person brushed by him, and he gave up his delusions of stalling. He had to just man up and face her.

Gwen's cubicle was the last in the long row of finance people. She was bent over her keyboard, a scowl on her pretty face. She was one of the few people who wore business attire on a daily basis and today's suit was a charcoal grey matched with a rose blouse. Her golden-blonde hair was pulled back in a severe, no-nonsense ponytail, lying pin-straight along her spine. She wore almost no makeup, but she didn't really need any, her clear skin and violet eyes were striking all on their own. Ryan wished she didn't scowl all the time, but he never dared say anything out loud to her. He liked his balls right where they were, thank you very much.

Her head came up as he approached her space, and her scowl deepened. He self-consciously touched his zipper and then straightened his spine. "Hi," he said, standing over her.

She looked up at him, took a second to check him out. "You don't look nearly as bad as I thought you would."

He laughed. He couldn't help himself. "Does that disappoint you?"

A small smile flickered across her lips, there and gone before it could even fully register. And that little flash of a grin was the reason why Ryan liked her. It was a thing most people didn't see because they never got past the frown. "Well, after that fight, I would have thought you'd show some bruising."

Oh, he was bruised all right. But not on the outside. "I'll try to get hit harder next time."

"You do that." She looked away from him, back to her computer. Her grimace reappeared instantly. She typed furiously on the keyboard, each stroke a pronounced tap. She glanced up at him again after a minute, clearly annoyed that he was still there. "What do you want, Ryan?"

"What do I want?" He pointed his index finger at her. "You're the one who wanted to see me."

She blinked once, pursed her lips. "Yes, I did." She gestured to the single guest chair resting against the far wall of the cubicle. "Well, don't just stand there hovering over me. Sit down."

"Right," Ryan said, as he took the chair and pulled up it next to her. Take two. "So, what's going on?"

She reached into a plastic set of shelves on her desk and retrieved a form. "Do you know what this is?"

He had no idea. He couldn't even see what it was. "No."

She held the page up, practically shaking it under his nose. "This is a project time allotment form."

He'd never heard of it. "Okay?"

She looked at him like he was an idiot. "It's what you're supposed to fill out for every single client you have. I need to track how much time you're spending on each aspect of a project and on which ones. The clients love it because it lets them see precisely what you're doing for them. The company uses it to see which projects are taking more time than others and set the bills accordingly."

He shrugged. "Makes sense."

She seemed to be waiting for him to say something more and when he didn't, she let out a long-suffering sigh. "Well, I don't have yours for the Betancourt website, but I'm sure you're still expecting to get paid."

"Oh," he said. Grace. His heart fell right down to his shoes.

"Yeah, oh," she said and handed him the wrinkled sheet. "Would you fill it out for me, please? By the end of the day? You can even do it online if you have something against paper."

He was proud of the work he'd done on Grace's site. He'd wanted to make her something stylized, something useful and functional that would help her out, but mostly he'd wanted to make her smile. He lived for her smile. He missed her so much. The ache in his heart was like a sucking, black abyss. He wasn't ever going to be right if he couldn't get her back. There had to be a way.

"Hello? Ryan? Can you hear me?"

Ryan forced himself back to the present and focused on Gwen. "I'm sorry, what was that?"

Her eyes narrowed. "What's wrong with you? No witty remark? No flirtatious comeback?"

He didn't know why he chose to tell her. Maybe he just needed to tell someone. Maybe he needed any help he could get. "I messed up and I lost—" *Everything.* "The girl I was seeing. Grace. She left me."

Gwen eased back in her chair, and for a change, there was concern on her face. "What happened?"

"I forgot that I invited another woman to the fight as well." He grimaced, saying it out loud. He knew how bad it was. "They kind of met there."

She rolled her eyes. "Come on, Ryan, what do you expect? This had to happen sooner or later. You're a total manslut."

He frowned at her. "I am not a slut."

She eyed him up and down. "Name one woman in this office you haven't thought about sleeping with."

He sputtered, but she had him. And they both knew it. "You make it sound so dirty."

"What you don't get, Ryan, is that when a woman sleeps with a charming man she finds attractive, she can't help but get expectations. Most people, when they sleep with someone, do it because they want something more. Or the relationship has progressed to the point where there is more." She leaned toward him, holding his gaze. "Not everyone takes things as casually as you do."

Something more. That was what he wanted. It was all lost now though. He sat up in the chair, trying to recover some semblance of his pride. "Grace is different."

"Why?" she asked, placing her chin in her palm. She looked as though she was genuinely interested in his reply. "How is she different? Because you haven't slept with her yet?"

He looked away.

"You have slept with her! You're terrible." She shook her head.

"I'm surprised you still care then."

He was offended, but he couldn't be. He remembered what the Ring Card Girl had said. He did sleep with people and not care. She was right. It was true. "I wanted it to be different. *I* wanted to be different." He bowed his head, defeated. "I wanted to be a nice guy for her."

She snorted. "Please."

"I'm in love with her, Gwen."

She burst out laughing, but stopped when she saw the expression on his face. "Really?"

"Yeah, really." And it was tearing him apart. "Come on, help me out. How can I get her back?"

The finance guru looked less than pleased to be having this conversation, but for some reason she decided to plow on. "Have you tried calling her?"

"Of course. I've called her, texted her, emailed her. She won't answer."

"I can't really blame her," she said under her breath. "You're going to have to do something really big." She tapped her chin, thinking it over. "Like you need to go to her place and hold a boombox up over your head outside her window."

He was not seeing the humor. "I think that's been done."

"You could write her a song or try serenading her or dedicating a play to her." She leaned forward, really getting into it now. "Ooo! Or you could get her some orange Tic Tacs."

He couldn't believe she was actually referencing all these movies. He would've never thought she had it in her. "I would've never taken you for a chick flick kind of woman."

She grimaced. "Shut up, Ryan. It's not like you don't know what I'm talking about."

He held up his hands in surrender. He couldn't lose her now. He needed her. She had to tell him what to do. He was at a total loss. "No, I hear you. I get it. A grand gesture. But this is real life, Gwen, and I need her back. What can I do?"

She sighed. "Groveling. You need to grovel and beg."

He winced. But he was desperate. Anything to get her back. "You think it'll work?"

"You really are serious about her," Gwen said quietly.

He nodded. "I am."

"Then, I think it's your only real option."

"Thanks, Gwen," he said, sincerely grateful for her help.

"Yeah, yeah," she said with a wave of her hand. "Now get out of my cubicle. Some of us actually work around here."

Chapter Eight

Seth stood at the edge of the cliff overlooking the torrid waters of the Atlantic Ocean. Wind whipped his dark hair around his handsome face. "I've never felt about anyone the way I feel about you," he said, standing close to Mia.

"Me either," she replied and pushed him off the cliff.

Grace sighed and held her finger down on the delete button. No matter how much she wanted to, she couldn't bring herself to kill Seth. He didn't deserve to suffer because his inspiration was a jackass. Seth was a nice guy, an honorable man, and her editor loved the character, loved the romantic set up, and was demanding more. Seth was in the Hamptons for the long haul.

She bowed her head and rubbed her tired eyes. The light of the computer screen was still bright behind her eyelids, and she squeezed her eyes shut to try to dispel some of the glare. The break in concentration allowed some of the feelings she had been trying so hard to suppress all week leak in. Anger, irritation, and most of all, heart-wrenching hurt racked her soul. She wasn't sure what galled her more, that he'd played her or that she'd fallen for it. When he'd told her he wanted her, she'd believed him. That was the worst part. It had meant so much to her and absolutely nothing to him. They were just words he whispered to whoever happened to be in his bed. Meaningless.

But a part of her refused to believe that. A small part of her held onto the memory of the look in his eyes when he'd said it, the way he'd made her feel. They'd made a real connection that night, something deep and powerful, and no matter how much she wanted to deny it, it was true. That look had been a promise all its own, saying more than words ever could. It made her want to believe that they could have something special, something lasting. It made her want to call him, talk to him, see him again. It made her long for him in the darkest hours of the night.

For the first time, in a long time, she wished she had someone to speak to, a friend to commiserate with. After she'd moved her father into Westview, she'd isolated herself so thoroughly, she didn't have many options. Tennyson came to mind, and she glanced at the phone, but made no move to pick it up. Ten had gotten her the appointment with Sharpe Designs. Complaining to him about Ryan might just land her web designer in a boatload of trouble. She doubted company policy allowed employees to sleep with their clients. She was furious and heartbroken, but she didn't want to get him fired. Besides, what would she even say? A man I slept with, who I had no business getting involved with anyway, used a tired old line with me in bed and I fell for it?

"Yeah, that's not happening," she said out loud and looked back at the computer screen. The cursor blinked endlessly, relentlessly, demanding that the blank page be filled. She rested her hands on the keyboard. This was her life. This was everything good and wonderful and true. It was what she loved to do. It was the only thing she needed. She couldn't believe she'd been willing to compromise it all for him.

She read over the words she'd written before her little flight of fancy and tugged on her lower lip as she tried to formulate where the scene would go. Seth and Mia were at the inn, alone in her office. He was trying to convince her to trust him, to let him help her find the murderer who'd struck during the blackout. Mia was reluctant to work with him, suspicious of his intentions. Seth had helped her in the past, but he had also done some dubious things that made Mia wonder about him. He was the classic bad boy archetype—handsome, charming, but also reckless, and more than a little bit dangerous. Mia liked him, maybe even lusted after him at this point, but he hadn't earned her trust yet. Still, she wasn't throwing him out of her office or anything, so something needed to happen next.

Grace let out a long breath and…

Nothing.

"Come on," she groaned. "What happens next?"

The hateful curser flashed on and on, and Grace clenched her jaw, willing the ideas to come. The work had been hard going lately, her emotions too tangled up to let her write with the freedom she had previously enjoyed, but she had no time for setbacks. She placed her hands on the keys and began to type.

Seth crossed the room, standing close before her. The heat of his body was a welcome and terrible distraction.

"Why are you even here?" Mia hissed at him, trying to put some space between them.

"I want to help."

Her eyes narrowed. "You're here because you're guilty."

"I'm here because

"Because I love you," Grace said to her empty apartment.

Everything in her recoiled at the admission, even as her heart screamed that it was true. She buried her face in her hands. That was no good. She never wanted to see him again. There was no way she could ever trust him. She would always wonder in the back of her mind if she really meant anything to him, and she couldn't live with that kind of constant doubt. It would drive her insane. She'd rather be alone.

Once again, that small, insistent part of her pointed out the look in his eyes when he'd held her. Just because it hadn't meant anything to him to sleep with the other woman, didn't mean he felt the same way when he slept with her.

Grace quickly pushed the thought aside. It was too arrogant to consider. There was nothing special about her, nothing that set her apart from the other woman in any significant way.

Unless maybe he loved her too.

She didn't have time to reflect on the ramifications of that little blockbuster of a thought because her email pinged, saving her from her own crazy speculations.

She clicked over and saw that it was from Ryan. Her heart lurched, stopped, beat wildly. She was going to ignore it, wanted to ignore it, but it was from his work account and the subject line read: Your Website. She opened the email and found just a few words and a link. *Your website is ready*, it said. *www.GraceBetancourt.com*

She clicked the link and gasped when the page loaded. It was breathtaking, and she couldn't help but be thrilled by the sight. It was everything she hoped for, the dark night, the unnamed menace, the warm and welcoming inn. The lake seemed to shimmer, and she almost thought she could see the stars twinkling. A bit of light in far corner caught her eye, and she looked closer at the image, her face almost touching the screen. There in the night sky was the sparkling tail of a comet, soaring close to the moon.

Emotion robbed her of breath. She'd looked up the myth the next day, the story behind the comet named for Endymion, the legendary shepherd and his beloved moon goddess, Selene. There was also a poem by John Keats, a beautiful story of the boy's epic quest for his true love. Both were tales of desire and longing, of trials faced and overcome.

The image on the screen held her gaze, her heart full of memories of that night. She'd known the instant she'd kissed him that getting involved with him was going to be dangerous. She'd never anticipated just how much though.

The alarm on her phone buzzed, and she glanced at the clock

on the computer. It was time to call it a day and go visit her dad. She was cautiously optimistic about his progress. Since getting out of the hospital, he seemed more lucid and in control. It was probably only temporary, another bad spell was mostly likely right around the corner, but she did enjoy it for the time being.

In twenty minutes, she was showered and ready to go. She chose a sundress for the day, a light lavender cotton dress that was both casual and chic. Maybe she'd drive a little further out on the island today after she saw her dad and visit the lake for old time's sake. It had been almost two years since her last trip there, and from what she could see out her apartment windows, it was shaping up to be a gorgeous day. A little escapade might be just the thing she needed to help soothe her weary, confused heart.

She bounced out of her apartment, down the stairs, and out onto the street. She stopped dead in her tracks when she caught sight of Ryan Granger leaning against a red sports coupé parked directly outside her building.

He gave her a crooked grin. "Hi."

"Hi," she replied softly. Why did her heart have to speed up at the sight of him, her arms long to hold him? Why did she have to love him? It was never going to work. She met his gaze and that look was there again, that wonderfully undefinable look that made her warm and chilled and giddy all at the same time. That look tested her will, but she straightened her spine, steeling herself against it. "I thought you were at your office? I got your email."

He sighed, looked away momentarily, then met her gaze again. "I miss you, Grace."

I miss you too! she wanted to scream, but she wasn't about to embarrass herself on a public street. She wanted to believe in him, she truly did, but it was hard to get past how much he'd hurt her. "We don't have anything to talk about, Ryan. And what are you doing here anyway? Have you been sitting outside my apartment all day?"

"No," he said. "I knew you'd be coming out about now. It's

Friday, the day you always visit your dad." He gestured to the car he was leaning on. "I thought I might give you a ride."

"Do you really tell every woman the same line?" she asked, her voice a pale whisper of its normal self.

His face fell, pain flashing across his handsome features. "I'm so sorry for what happened, more than you could ever know. I'm not a nice guy. I told you that. And she was not the first woman I've slept with and not known her name." He pushed himself off the car and took a step closer to her. "But she will be the last. I may be a lot of things, but I'm no cheater. And I only want you, Grace. No one else." He took a deep breath. "You mean so much to me. I—" He paused, looked at the ground, and then back to her. "I want to be a nice guy for you." He gave her a tight smile. "But I don't know how. I'm going to need a lot of help."

Weak. She was a weak woman. She ached for him. He was so close. It would be so easy to collapse in his arms, forgive him everything, and let him whisk her away with a promise and a kiss. "You haven't answered my question."

He took another step toward her. "No. The words may have been the same, but the intention was not." He seemed to struggle with himself, and his Adam's apple bobbed in his throat as he swallowed hard. "It could never be the same. You're the only one that I love."

His words hit her square in the gut. She shook her head, denying everything, her brain fizzling with pure sensory overload. "You don't mean that."

"I *do* mean that." He stood close enough now that she could feel the heat of his body. He reached out and brushed his finger-tips down the back of her arms. The light caress set her bare skin alight with heated chills. She tried to look away, but he caught her chin and met her gaze. "I love you, Grace."

How could she resist him? He was everything she wanted. He was all that she wanted. She had to forgive him. She had to take a chance and trust him. She was helpless not to. "You're ridiculous."

A wide grin broke out on his handsome face and her heart sped up in her chest. "Does that mean you love me too?"

Oh, no, he wasn't getting off that easy. "It means I'm willing to recognize your flaws and move forward with you on a probationary basis." She touched his cheek. "Because I'm totally, crazy in love with you."

She allowed him to take her into his arms and didn't resist when his mouth found hers for a long, deep, toe-curling kiss. A warming sensation glided down her body from her lips to her core, and her arms wound around his neck, hugging him close. The familiar feel of his heart beating against hers heated her in ways beyond any simple lust could manage. She was awash in a heady torrent of relief, pleasure, desire, and most importantly, love. This was the man she wanted to spend her forever with.

He pulled back with a soft sigh and met her gaze, mirth dancing in his eyes. "You thought about killing me, didn't you? Planned out all the ways I could meet an untimely demise?"

She laughed. How could she not? He was ridiculous. And he knew her very well. "Yeah, of course I did."

He touched his forehead to hers, kissed her lightly on the lips. "You look nice." He dipped his head to kiss her throat and her stomach fluttered. "You smell nice." He ran his fingers through her hair. "Are you ready to go?"

"Yes," she said, suddenly guilty. She'd forgotten all about her father. She was a horrible, selfish daughter. "I need to leave now or I'm going to be late."

He took her hand and escorted her around the car to the passenger's side. "Your chariot awaits, M'lady."

She lingered outside the car, chewing on her lower lip. "I'd like you to meet my dad," she said, and plowed on before she could second-guess herself with too many neurotic, anxious thoughts. "He probably won't understand that he's meeting you though."

Ryan took both her hands in his. "I'd love to meet him."

She had to swallow back the emotion that rose in her throat before she could speak again. "Then let's go."

He helped her into the car, and they hit the road, heading out to Long Island. Traffic was heavy, everyone bailing out of work early to abandon the city and get to the beaches and their summer homes, their weekend getaways. They got snarled up about halfway to their destination, caught in bumper to bumper traffic that extended for miles and miles.

"I know this probably isn't the best time to bring this up," Ryan said, glancing over at her then back at the road. "But I want to be with you, Grace, and I need to see you more than once a week. I understand you have work to do, but being with you part time is not going to be enough for me."

Grace had willfully chosen to ignore the demands of her writing schedule and what it would mean to actively be with him. It was not an issue she cared to talk about, and thinking about it only made her nerves buzz with stress, but it was something that had to be addressed. She was never going to be able to be with him every night. The only way she was going to make him understand was to be totally, bluntly, honest with him. "Ryan, this place where my father is staying—it's not cheap. Insurance doesn't cover the cost. If I don't write, I'm not going to be able to afford it. I won't let him be put in some state institution." She shivered at the ghastly thought. "Never." Her jaw clenched. "Writing has to be my number one priority."

He was quiet as the traffic rolled a few inches forward. "I can help you out," he said finally.

She shook her head. "No, Ryan—"

"I can," he insisted. "I make good money at Sharpe. And I'll only be making more as I take on more of my own clients. You don't have to carry the burden all on your own."

His sweetness was overwhelming. "I can't let you do that." She chuckled softly. "We haven't even been on a single real date yet, there's no way I'm going to let you start paying my rent or something else equally as insane. We have to take this slow. One step at a time."

"Okay," he said, and she could tell from the tone of his voice this was an issue he was not going to let drop. They would be discussing it again—probably over and over again. "But I still want more of your time."

Once again she was faced with a choice. Could she compromise her entire life for him? Did she want to? "Maybe we can work out a schedule."

He laughed and shook his head. "Do you ever just go with the flow, Grace? Take a chance, follow a whim?" He reached over the gear shift and took her hand. "I want to be with you all night, every night, but I understand you need your time. Let's see where this takes us, live in the moment, all those clichés." The side-glance he flashed her was full of innuendo and wicked promise. "Let's have a little fun."

The relationship hadn't even begun, and she was already in trouble. How was she ever going to survive it? There was no way she could tell him no. "Okay."

He smiled and she didn't think she'd ever seen a man nearly as beautiful as Ryan Granger. "Good. Let's start tonight."

She laughed as the traffic cleared out before them, allowing them to continue on to Westview. "I was thinking of going out to the lake tonight. Maybe walking around a bit. Does that sound like something you'd want to do?"

"Yes," he said, lacing his fingers through hers. "It absolutely does."

The exits flew by outside the window, the familiar route filled with promise rather than the usual heartbreaking routine. Ryan released her hand to better navigate the pitfalls of the highway. She looked over at him, studying his profile. "What ever happened with your mother?"

His eyebrows shot up at the sudden change in conversation. "What do you mean?"

"She didn't stay broken forever, did she? I mean, is she all right now? What happened?"

He glanced over at her, then quickly away, but not so fast that she wasn't able to see the sadness in his eyes. "No, she eventually got better." He swallowed. "When she met someone else."

Grace nodded as the quiet stretched out between them. It wasn't uncomfortable, but it was tense. She waited, hoping that he would continue, maybe let her in a little bit. She needed him to share this part of himself with her, especially since he was going to meet her father.

"That relationship lasted three years, and when it ended, she was just as devastated." He paused. "Maybe even more so."

Miles rolled away under the car. The yellow line was a blur in the corner of Grace's eye.

"She's on husband number three now, and if I let myself think about it too much, it eats a hole in my stomach." He worried his lower lip with his teeth. "For the first time ever, I'm not in Philly. I don't know how she's going to cope this time."

"Maybe there won't be a 'this time.'"

Ryan let out a bitter huff. "There's always a this time."

"That isn't real love, Ryan."

He opened his mouth, closed it, then looked over at her. His face softened when he met her gaze. "Yes, I'm beginning to see that." He took her hand again before turning back to the road. "I also finally get why she keeps searching for it." He gently caressed her knuckles. "That wasn't something I ever understood before."

"Well, you know, if you do go back, at all, for whatever reason…" She stopped her rambling gush of words and gave his hand a gentle squeeze, hoping her touch would convey all the things she meant to say. "I'd like to go with you."

He went very still beside her, the impact of her words creating a heavy tension between them. For a long moment he just drove, silently holding her hand, until finally he glanced away from the windshield to look directly at her. "I'd like that."

She nodded, too overcome to trust her own voice. He was willing to let her in, to take down a few of the walls around his

115

heart for her—just as she had done for him by allowing him to join her today. That one, little sentence meant everything. It was exactly what she always dreamed true love would be.

They arrived at Westview Gardens a little while later and parked in the visitors' lot. Nerves assaulted her as they crossed the grounds toward her father's building. Introducing a boy to her dad had always been a terrifying experience, but this time it was even worse. This time it actually mattered, regardless of whether her father remembered him or not. Today she was going to introduce him to the man she loved.

She entered her father's room first, checking to see if he was awake. He smiled when he saw her, and she was pleased to see that his eyes were clear and focused. "Hi, Dad."

"Gracie!" he said, opening his arms to her.

She crossed the room and hugged him tight. How she wished it was always this way with him. His lucid moments were so infrequent now. She cherished them whenever she could.

"Gracie?" her dad asked, looking over her shoulder. "Who's the man in the doorway?"

Here we go, she thought and forced a smile on her face. Just be cool. "Dad, I'd like you to meet Ryan." She held out her hand to Ryan, calling him over. "Ryan, this is my dad."

Her father held out his hand, a polite smile on his face. So far, so good. "Hello, Ryan."

"Hello, sir," Ryan said, shaking his hand. "It's good to meet you."

"Ryan made me a gorgeous website," she said. "I love it."

Her father nodded, absorbing that tidbit of information. "That's great, honey."

Yup, great. She took a deep breath. "And we're, um, kind of… seeing one another."

"Kind of seeing one another?" her father said, turning back to her. "What exactly does that mean?"

The jovialness in his voice both elevated and crushed her heart all at the same time. It was the same tone he'd used every time she'd brought a new boy home for inspection. "Um, it means, that he is, ahhh…" A wild blush heated her cheeks, and she sighed. In love or not, it seemed that she was forever going to have articulation issues.

"I'm her boyfriend, sir," Ryan interjected. He flashed Grace a devilish grin. "Boyfriend. I think that was the word you were looking for."

She wasn't sure how it was possible, but she wanted to both die and jump for joy right there in her father's private room.

Her father's gaze was suddenly very intent on Ryan. "Is that so?"

"It is, sir. I'm a very lucky man."

"Yes you are," her father agreed.

Something passed over her father's face then, something very much like a cloud drifting over the sun and his eyes went a hazy shade of faded grey. Grace held her breath, preparing herself for the worst. Her throat tightened, but when he blinked again, she saw that he was still himself.

"Sit down, Ryan," her father said, gesturing toward the chairs by the open bay window. He affected a stern face, but Grace knew it was all for show. "I want to hear all about your plans with my daughter."

Ryan laughed as he brought both the chairs to her father's bedside. "I think my number one objective is to get Grace to have a bit more fun. She takes herself far too seriously."

"Don't I know it," her dad replied. "She has ever since she was a little girl."

"Hey!" she said, trying hard to sound offended, but she was smiling too widely to actually pull it off. "I'm standing right here, guys."

Ryan gave her a saucy wink and held out a chair for her. She sat down between the two most important men in her life, settling in for what she was sure was going to be an amusingly embarrassing conversation. Later, when they were done visiting her dad, she was going to spend the night with the man she loved. Life wasn't perfect, but it could be pretty good sometimes.